THE FLYING WAGON

Other books by I. J. Parnham:

THE FLYING WAGON

•

I. J. Parnham

AVALON BOOKS
NEW YORK

Published by Thomas Bouregy & Co., Inc.
160 Madison Avenue, New York, NY 10016

Library of Congress Cataloging-in-Publication Data

Parnham, I. J.
    The flying wagon / I. J. Parnham.
        p. cm.
    ISBN 978-0-8034-9871-6 (acid-free paper)
    I. Title.

    PS3616.A763F55 2007
    813'.6—dc22
                                    2007024711

PRINTED IN THE UNITED STATES OF AMERICA
ON ACID-FREE PAPER
BY HADDON CRAFTSMEN, BLOOMSBURG, PENNSYLVANIA

Chapter One

Jim Broughton opened the shutters and favored the bank's first customer, Walter Smithies, with a thin smile.

"What you want?" he asked.

"I'd like to make a deposit." Walter slammed a bulging bag on the counter.

Jim eyed the bag, then prodded it with a steady rhythm.

"How much?"

"No idea."

With a pained wince, Jim upended the bag. A heap of pennies grew, then grew some more until the edges spread out to fill the counter and the heap resembled a small mountain. He shuffled through the

1

coins finding only pennies. From under his teller's rim, he glanced at Walter.

"Pennies, you've got nothing but pennies?"

"That's right," Walter said, tucking his thumbs into his waistcoat. "Been collecting them for nigh on twelve years."

"And you chose today and me to bank them with?"

"That's right."

Jim took a deep breath, then pushed the heap to the side of the counter to clear a space. With steady care, he fingered one penny at a time across the counter.

"One, two, three, four, five—"

"Hurry up there in front," the second customer, Miles Parson, shouted, peering over Walter's shoulder.

Jim pushed his counted pennies back into the main heap and looked up.

"Wait your turn. I'm going as fast as I can." Jim slid the coins across the counter again. "One, two, three, four, five—"

"Why are you starting again?" Walter muttered. "I'll be here all day."

Jim winced and swung his counted pennies back.

"Because that man interrupted me and I lost count. One, two, three, four, five—"

Walter leaned on the counter. "You ain't the normal teller, are you?"

Jim rubbed his eyes, then swiped the coins back into the heap.

"I ain't. One, two, three, four, five—"

"Well, I've got some advice for you. If you keep restarting—"

"And if you keep interrupting . . ." Jim widened his eyes and glanced at the clock behind him.

"I was going to say that when Matlock counts coins he puts them into piles of five, then if he loses track, he doesn't have to restart."

"I ain't Matlock," Jim snapped. "One, two, three, four, five—"

"Perhaps you should get Matlock out here. He could do this a whole lot faster."

"He ain't here. One, two, three, four, five"—Jim glanced up at Walter but Walter had clamped his mouth shut—"*six*, seven, eight—"

"Where is he?"

Jim swiped his counted coins back into the heap and slammed his fist on the counter, rattling the heap.

"I ain't no teller. I'm a U.S. marshal from Westside Creek. I've come to White Springs to relieve Matlock because I reckon there's going to be a bank raid."

Walter gulped and glanced around. "There's going to be a bank raid?"

"Keep your voice down." Jim took a deep breath. "One, two, three . . ."

Miles tapped Walter's shoulder. "How far has he got?"

"He's up to six, now seven," Walter said.

Miles considered the heap of pennies. "This is going to take forever. Can't he fetch Matlock to help?"

"No. Matlock ain't around." Walter cupped his hand beside his mouth. "There's going to be a bank raid."

"A bank raid!"

Jim broke off from his counting at twenty and looked up.

"Will you please be quiet." When both men turned to the front, he swung the counted coins back into the heap and sighed. "One, two, three . . ."

Miles waited until the count reached fifty, then wandered outside, muttering. The other customer in the queue followed him out.

An hour later, and after three different counting tactics and several more unserved and unsatisfied customers, Jim looked up and blew out his cheeks.

"One thousand, two hundred and sixty-three," he said, a smile emerging as he flexed his tired fingers.

Walter snorted. "I made it one thousand, two hundred and sixty-two."

"I thought you didn't know"—Jim grabbed a penny and hurled it over the top of the serving hatch, where it rattled to a halt in the corner—"our counts are in agreement."

With much grumbling, Walter left the bank.

When the door closed, Jim's deputy, Lloyd Henderson, wandered in from the back room and stood beside Jim until he looked up.

"There's going to be a bank raid," he murmured.

"And what was I supposed to say?"

"Anything but that."

"But he annoyed me."

"You're a teller. And that's what you have to put up with."

"I'm a lawman, not this . . . this teller." Jim threw his cap to the floor and kicked it against the wall.

"When you're serving customers, you're a teller. When Van Romalli raids the bank, you're a lawman."

"Then I hate to say this, but I hope Romalli hurries up and raids."

As Lloyd nodded, Walter Smithies dashed back in.

"Help, help!" he shouted.

Jim wrapped his arms around the heap of counted pennies.

"I ain't recounting this money."

"I don't want you to. Someone's raided Miles' store next door." Walter dashed outside, urging the lawmen to follow him out.

Lloyd and Jim debated whether this was another one of Van Romalli's infamous distractions, but when Walter poked his head around the door and demanded that they hurry, they followed him outside and into the adjoining store. As they dashed in, guns drawn, Walter was slipping a gag from the tied-up storekeeper's mouth.

"What happened?" Jim asked.

"That bank raider you were expecting came here

instead," Miles whined, then dry spat to the side to clear his throat.

"How do you know he was a bank raider?"

"After you said there'd be a bank raid I kept my cash, but this man followed me back from the bank, knocked me out, and stole my money."

Jim shook his head. "The customer who left the bank after you was a woman."

"Then *he* was waiting outside, but it don't matter. He stole everything."

"What did he look like?"

"He knocked me out from behind. I never saw him."

With his face set in a sneer, Jim considered the ransacked store, then drew Lloyd aside.

"Van Romalli?" he asked.

"Got to be. That man never does what you expect him to do."

"Come on, then," Jim said as he headed for the door. "He won't have got far."

"You reckon it'll do any good?" Lloyd asked, hurrying after Jim. "Romalli's always two steps ahead of us and I reckon we'll just be chasing phantoms for the rest of the day."

"I reckon that too." Jim stopped in the doorway. "But what else can we do but chase after him?"

The buckboard appeared to have been abandoned at the side of the trail. The wheel tracks leading toward it lurched across the trail and the buckboard itself stood at a crazy angle with two wheels buried deep in a wheel rut.

Fifty yards from the buckboard, Randolph Mc-Dougal pulled back on the reins, slowing the wagon he was driving, then glanced at Fergal O'Brien, who sat beside him, but Fergal was already leaning forward and peering around at the surrounding grasslands.

The only movement came from the buckboard's threadbare cloth awning as it rustled in the breeze, and from the moth-eaten, bow-legged and bow-chested bay that bustled against its rigging as it stared longingly at the grass beside the trail.

As they passed, Randolph ran his gaze over the derelict buckboard, confirming that he could see nobody inside or nearby.

They were thirty miles out of White Springs, and Harvest Pass was another twenty miles away. In White Springs, Randolph had learned that the trail between these two towns was bandit country, and that the infamous outlaw Van Romalli was working the area.

Fergal and Randolph were traveling showmen, displaying a dubious collection of *homemade*, authentic, historical memorabilia and selling an even more dubious universal remedy to cure all ills. But despite the lack of rich pickings for an outlaw like Van Romalli, Randolph was already on alert for potential danger. Even so, he ignored Fergal's grumbling and, ten yards on, halted the wagon, then jumped down.

He stalked toward the abandoned buckboard, walking sideways with his Peacemaker drawn and held up beside his cheek. The bay considered him with sullen disinterest.

"Help!"

The plea came from the long grass beside the trail.

"Could be a trap," Fergal said, peering round the side of the wagon.

"Don't be so suspicious," Randolph snorted. "And that voice was a woman's."

"Could still be a trap."

"If you're so worried, stay here."

Randolph paced from the trail and waded into the head-high grass. He heard Fergal jumping down and pattering after him, but he didn't look back. Instead, he craned his neck to see over the grass and so ensure he had advance warning of whatever might be awaiting him.

He broke through the grass to emerge on to an area of bare soil. Dotted about were boulders and beyond was a creek that arced back and forth like a sidewinder until it disappeared into the low heat haze. Flies buzzed around him, the sound close and insistent.

But then a whimper sounded, coming from behind the boulder furthest to his right.

Randolph took a deep breath, then glanced over his shoulder to direct Fergal to stay where he was on the edge of the grass area. Fergal returned a shrug, indicating that staying away from trouble was something he never needed encouragement to do.

Walking sideways, Randolph paced in a circle, giving the boulder a wide berth, but as the other side swung into his view, he saw outstretched legs then a woman. She was leaning back against the boulder. Dirt coated her torn dress. An ugly bruise marred her cheek.

But what shocked Randolph the most was that this was a woman he recognized—Morgana Sullivan, a woman who had double-crossed Fergal and stolen a supply of his universal remedy six months earlier.

She cringed as she saw Randolph, but on her lap was a rifle and she snapped her arm up to aim it directly at him. Although the barrel shook, from ten yards away Randolph didn't doubt that she could blast him in two with even a poorly directed shot.

"What you want?" she screeched, with anger and fear in her voice.

"The remedy you stole off us would be a good start."

"Look at me," she said, gritting her teeth. "Do I look as if I can help you with that right now?"

Randolph considered her disheveled state and pained expression. For the last six months he'd listened to Fergal's litany of ever more inventive punishments he'd mete out if they ever found this woman again. But now that they had, Randolph found he couldn't bring himself to add to her distress.

"Perhaps you can't," he said, fighting down his anger so that he could use his softest voice. "But maybe I can . . . I can help you first."

Hope flashed in her eyes before she blinked it away.

"If you're lying, I know how to use this rifle."

"I don't doubt it." Moving slowly, Randolph holstered his gun, then lifted his hands high. "But we can discuss what you did to us later. For now let us help you."

"We?" She flicked her head to the side, seeing Fergal loitering on the edge of the clear area. She swung the rifle toward him, then snapped it back to Randolph. "You got any more men hiding out there?"

"There's just the two of us." Randolph smiled. "Are you in pain?"

"Yeah. I'm hurt real bad." She gestured toward several spots about her body while wincing.

"As you know, Fergal here is a medical man . . ." Randolph glanced at Fergal, then shrugged. "Well, he has a medical bag. Perhaps he can help you with one of his special tonics."

"I'm not risking that," she snorted, but then lowered the rifle to her lap.

Fergal scurried across the clear area to join Randolph now that she'd lowered the rifle. He set his feet wide and raised a finger. His hunched posture suggested he was settling in for a long argument about either the property she'd stolen off him or his tonic's merits, but Randolph slapped his shoulder.

"She don't need an argument right now." He stared at Fergal until he provided a reluctant nod.

With both men now providing encouraging smiles, Morgana propped the rifle against the boulder, then staggered to her feet. Although she swayed, Randolph didn't move to help her, preferring not to frighten her any more than he already had.

She provided a quick shrug. "I'm sorry about—"

"That don't matter right now." He gestured back to the trail. "What happened here?"

Morgana flinched and glanced around her. "Does that mean you haven't found Martha, my friend?"

"No, just you."

Morgana gulped then pointed. "She ran off that way toward the creek."

"And who was she running from?"

"I . . . I don't know who he was. He was just this outlaw."

"Van Romalli?"

Something flashed in her eyes, perhaps fear, perhaps recognition of the name, but she blinked then looked away from Randolph.

"I . . . I . . . I don't know. I shot at him, but he . . .

he chased Martha away." She closed her eyes a moment. "And he hasn't come back."

"How long ago?"

She fingered her scalp, wincing. "Not too sure. I think I banged my head and passed out for a while."

"Don't worry. I'll find her. You stay here and let Fergal look after you."

Randolph mustered a wide smile, then flashed a warning glance at Fergal, silently ordering him not to upset her by demanding their property back just yet. When Fergal returned a nod, he headed toward the creek. Within a few paces, he found a line of footprints. They were wide-spaced, but deep and small, suggesting to him that a woman had made them and that she was running quickly down the slope towards the creek.

Randolph searched for her pursuer's prints but didn't find any. But he followed her prints as they veered to the side, then ran along the side of the creek. Numerous boulders and hollows were ahead, and Randolph took his time as he edged into each hollow or around each boulder. Each time he expected to confront a sight he didn't want to see, but each time he found only more prints.

Then the trail took a sharp turn toward the creek and across a patch of mud before they disappeared into the water.

Randolph climbed on to a tuft of elevated ground and stared across the creek, hoping to see whether

Martha had emerged on the other side. But although the creek was only thirty feet wide and he had a good view of the sandy soil on the other side, he couldn't see any prints there.

And neither could he see any sign of her pursuer's prints on either side.

"Find anything?" a voice demanded from behind him.

Randolph turned at the hip towards the speaker. His Peacemaker cleared leather, but even as he raised his arm, he noted it was Fergal. So, by the time he'd fully turned, he was already smiling.

"Never sneak up on me."

"I wasn't sneaking. You should have been listening more carefully." Fergal joined Randolph on the tuft of ground and replicated his steady gaze over both sides of creek. "It's as if she just disappeared."

"Or swam away."

"Or drowned."

"Stop being pessimistic."

"I'm not. I'm being realistic."

Randolph sighed. "How's Morgana?"

"I persuaded her to drink a bottle of my tonic, so she's perking up nicely."

"That won't last," Randolph murmured to himself.

"What?"

"I said that she's a fortunate woman. But we can't go back without finding out what happened to her friend."

Fergal turned on the spot, tracing Martha's route along the side of the creek, then, with a hand to his brow, peered into the distance. He shook his head.

"We need to know everything that happened here. Then we'll all search along the creek. And we will find her."

With that agreement, they turned and retraced the footprints back to the boulder where they'd left Morgana, but as they climbed up from the creek, Randolph saw that she was no longer there.

"I hope she hasn't wandered too far," he said, peering around. "We don't want to be searching for two women."

Fergal slid to a halt, slapped his forehead, then broke into a run.

"We won't have to," he shouted over his shoulder. "I know where *they* are."

Randolph watched Fergal round the boulder and hurry out of sight into the long grass, then shrugged and dashed after him, but as he bounded through the grass, he saw confirmation of what Fergal had just realized.

Their wagon had gone.

Randolph ran on for another ten paces, then slowed to a halt at a spot where he could see down the trail.

Two hundred yards ahead was their wagon, containing everything that they owned, and it was trundling away.

Morgana was peering around the side of the wagon at them. Her form was receding down the trail and she was already too far away for Randolph to discern her expression.

But she did have the courtesy to wave.

Chapter Two

The moth-eaten bay was wheezing again. Randolph shook the reins, encouraging the horse to speed up, but it plodded along the trail at a pace only marginally faster than he could walk, when he wasn't in a hurry, and if he had both legs tied together.

With no choice, Randolph and Fergal had commandeered Morgana's buckboard, but aside from discovering that it was debatable whether the horse would collapse before the buckboard fell apart, they'd only gained a way of getting to Harvest Pass—albeit slowly. And at this speed, Morgana would be getting farther away with every pace.

She had taken everything they owned: The supply of universal remedy bottles, the authentic display of

16

historic memorabilia, the wagon, and with it any chance of them making a living.

But from the set of their jaws, Fergal and Randolph conveyed to the world that every slow pace onward strengthened their resolve that they'd reclaim their property in a way that'd make the bushwhacker regret ever tangling with them.

But no matter how resolute they were, it didn't help to speed the slow horse. So, the sun was already dipping towards the horizon when their dawdling pursuit trundled them into Harvest Pass. It was a large frontier town. The railroad had arrived and the town had burst out in all directions in a manner that from outside the town appeared random, but which, as they reached the main road, proved to have a block structure.

On the edge of town, they pulled up outside a stable, or to be more precise, the horse livened up for the first time and dragged the buckboard to the trough then began guzzling water, forcing them to stop there.

Randolph gazed along the main road, then jumped down.

"I'll ask around and see if anyone's seen Morgana pass through," he said.

Fergal nodded, but on noticing that two men were chatting outside the stable, he grabbed his medical bag and removed two bottles of his universal remedy.

"And I'll start to rebuild our finances," he said, grinning.

Randolph provided a quick nod, then stood back to let Fergal make his approach to these people before he questioned them.

Fergal shook the bottles causing the amber liquid inside to sparkle in the reddened rays of the lowering sun.

"Welcome, friends!" he shouted, throwing his thin arms wide, revealing his bright green waistcoat. "Would you like to buy a tonic?"

The two men continued talking then flinched on realizing that Fergal had been addressing them, and turned.

"What does it do?" the clean-shaven of the two men asked.

"It's a universal remedy. No injury is so bad, no ailment is so painful, no condition is so embarrassing that this amber liquid cannot cure."

"Sounds good, but I ain't got anything wrong with me."

"Then it'll cure you of that."

The man stared back, his brow furrowing as he probably tried to deduce whether he'd heard this right, then shrugged.

But the bearded man paced forward. "I've got me a painful boil. Will it cure that?"

"It sure will. It is a universal remedy and it will cure anything. And all for one dollar."

"You got proof it'll work?"

Fergal shook the bottle and favored the man with his most generous smile.

"You can buy a bottle, and if it doesn't cure your boil within a week, I'll give you your money back."

The bearded man eyed the bow-legged bay, probably weighing up how far it could get in a week, then shook his head.

"You got proof *before* I buy a bottle."

"I reckon so." Fergal glanced around, but then flinched as he apparently noticed Randolph for the first time. He pointed at him. "Young man, you seem to have plenty of ills."

Randolph furrowed his brow, then turned to face the potential customers.

"Yeah, I've got plenty of ills," he said, forcing a pained smile as he tried to put as much enthusiasm into his performance as he could. He removed his hat, then hunched his shoulders and shuffled from side to side. "I'm a poor man, but if I had me a dollar to pay for this stranger's tonic, I sure would buy a bottle to cure me of 'em."

"Oh, you would, would you?" Fergal said, holding the bottle aloft. "And what's wrong with you?"

Randolph rubbed his chin as he considered the hundreds of ailments he'd claimed to have suffered from over the last few years—before Fergal had *cured* him—then settled for a new one.

"I'm deaf."

"You're deaf?" Fergal intoned.

"Sure am."

"And that means you can't hear a thing?"

"Nope."

"And how long have you suffered from an affliction that means you can't hear anything anyone says to you?"

"All my life. I just can't hear—" Randolph winced. He glanced at the expectant potential customers, then at the glaring Fergal. "I just can't hear anything that you're saying on account of me being deaf."

Fergal cracked a smile. "But if you were to drink my tonic, for free, you would be cured."

"What?"

"You," the bearded man shouted, "would be cured if you drank his tonic."

"Nope," Randolph said, "I still can't hear nothing anybody's saying."

Fergal jumped down from the buckboard and pushed the tonic into Randolph's hand.

Randolph glanced at the tonic, then mimed being shocked by opening his mouth wide and staggering back a pace.

"Are you really so generous as to give a poor man a free bottle of tonic to cure his affliction?"

"I sure am!" Fergal shouted, then lowered his voice so that only Randolph could hear. "And hurry up and drink it. You ain't that good an actor."

Randolph nodded and stood before the customers with the tonic cupped in his hand, then slipped out the stopper and put the bottle to his lips. He took a deep breath then sipped the tonic. He winced as his tongue shrank back, rebelling against the rotted polecat taste. But then a sly grin appeared and, to avoid drinking the rest of the foul brew, he emptied the bottle into his right ear, then shook away the excess and put on his largest smile.

"Well?" Fergal asked.

"I heard that!" Randolph shouted, opening his eyes wide. "Say something else!"

"It's a miracle," Fergal proclaimed, throwing his arms wide.

"And I heard that too."

As Randolph danced his usual celebratory jig, Fergal turned to the bearded man.

"There, I told you that it works."

"And I heard—"

"Enough," Fergal grunted then shook the other bottle. "So, do you want to buy a bottle?"

"I sure will." The man took the bottle. As he fished in his pocket for money, he held the bottle up to the light to consider it, then frowned and withdrew his hand. "But I've already got a bottle of this. It ain't a universal remedy. It's a universal cleaner."

"It is not a cleaner," Fergal muttered, his eyes flaring, but Randolph stopped celebrating his sudden ability to hear and patted the bearded man's arm.

"Where did you buy a bottle of this *cleaner*?" he asked.

The man pointed to a junction about halfway down the main road, beside the bank, after which Fergal snatched back the bottle.

"Young man," he said, turning to Randolph, "as I have now cured you of your deafness, would you consider joining me—"

Randolph dragged Fergal round and pointed him at his ex-customers, who had returned to their conversation and were showing no interest in whatever story Fergal was about to concoct. Fergal nodded and jumped on the buckboard, leaving Randolph to drag the bay away from the trough. At the usual slow pace, they headed down the road to the junction.

When they pulled up at the corner, Randolph saw that their wagon *was* standing at the far end of the road. Randolph glanced at Fergal, but Fergal was already rolling his shoulders and snorting his breath through his nostrils.

"You reckon we should see if there's a lawman in town?" Randolph asked.

"Nope, that woman is the kind of foe even I can take on. Come on. We're getting our wagon back."

"And getting rid of this moth-eaten horse." Randolph shook the reins, but the horse just looked over its shoulder and considered him with an appraising eye. For long moments, they shared eye contact. "I mean, and returning this noble beast to its rightful owner."

The horse returned to looking down the road and headed off at a speed that was almost up to walking pace.

As they trundled down the road, he saw that Morgana stood on the front of the wagon facing a circle of people as she presumably sold Fergal's tonic. Randolph couldn't help but notice that she was no longer disheveled and all signs of her former apparent distress had gone. He pulled back on the reins, but even before the buckboard had stopped, Fergal was alighting.

"And what do you think you're doing?" Fergal demanded as he stomped to a halt before his former wagon.

Morgana looked over the shoulders of her circle of customers and her gaze didn't flicker with even a moment's concern as she just smiled.

"And how can I help you?"

"You know exactly what you can do."

"Always pleased to meet a new customer." She held up a bottle of Fergal's amber universal remedy. "Would you like to buy a bottle of my cleaning liquid?"

"Cleaning liquid?" Fergal spluttered, staggering back a pace so that he stumbled into the advancing Randolph.

"Yes. I sell a universal cleaner to remove all stains. No mark is so deep, no stain is so large, no blemish is so embarrassing that my amber liquid cannot clean."

"Cleaning? Cleaning! Clean—" Fergal waved his arms above his head as he battled to form the right words to convey the insult she'd just delivered.

"Yeah, and it sure works." She held up a towel, half of which was mud-coated, the other half being clean. "And I can prove it."

"You not only stole my wagon, stole my display of authentic historical memorabilia, and stole my tonic, but now you're . . . you're selling my tonic as a cleaning product!"

Morgana darted her head back, frowning. "What do you mean about stealing *your* wagon?"

"That is my wagon," Fergal screeched, pointing, "and that is my universal remedy and that is my wagon. And did I say that that's my wagon?"

"You did, but I don't understand what you mean."

"Then understand this." Fergal set his feet wide. "You have precisely three seconds to get down the road and reclaim your moldering buckboard and your bow-legged horse or I'll do something that no lady should ever have to witness."

Morgana placed the bottle and towel on the seat behind her.

"And you have precisely three seconds to get

down the road and get on *your* buckboard or I'll do something that no man should ever have to witness."

"And what could you possibly do that'll stop me reclaiming my wagon?"

Morgana set her hands on her hips and raised her chin.

"One, two, *three*." Morgana looked down at Fergal with her eyebrows raised and her eyes blazing, and when Fergal just returned her gaze, she rolled her shoulders, then threw her arms wide.

Then she screamed at the top of her voice, the reverberations being loud enough to rock Fergal back on his heels and knock his hat to the ground. He rescued his hat and stood but still the screaming continued.

Her customers backed away to get out of the eardrum-splitting zone while they waited for her to run out of breath. But she appeared to have an inexhaustible lung capacity and everyone had to either stick their fingers in their ears or take refuge in the nearest buildings. And when it ended, one of her customers was impressed enough to burst into applause.

"That man is right," Fergal said, then, along with Randolph, waggled a finger in his ear to confirm that the ringing he was still hearing was just the after-effects and that she wasn't still screaming. "That was an impressive performance."

"I thought so too. You want another burst?"

Fergal returned to stand before her and forced a smile.

"I'd prefer not to, but now that you've frightened away your customers, we can talk in private and you can stop pretending. You have stolen my property." He beckoned Randolph to join him. "My friend here is a gentle man, but even so, I suggest you give it back before he gives you a whole heap of trouble."

Morgana shrugged. "Then if you want plain speaking, I'll give you some. Your cleaning product is—"

"It is not a cleaning product. It is a genuine universal remedy to cure all ills."

"If you say so, but either way, I'm selling it as a cleaning product and it's selling well. So, I have no intention of giving up your wagon and, unless you leave, I'll do something you won't enjoy, *again*." She threw open her mouth, but then closed it as Randolph and Fergal danced back before the onslaught started. "But maybe I won't have to. The law's arriving."

Fergal glanced over his shoulder. A man with a star was striding toward them. He and Randolph turned to face him.

"At last," Fergal said, urging Sheriff Johnson to hurry with a frantic hand gesture. "This here woman has—"

An ear-splitting screech erupted from behind him, the shock tumbling him to his knees and forcing the lawman to skid to a halt. He edged forward with his fingers in his ears until he stood beside Fergal, and presently the noise petered out.

"What seems to be the . . . ?" The sheriff patted his right ear, then continued. "What's happening here?"

Fergal swung his arm up and, with a trembling finger, pointed at Morgana.

"This here woman stole my wagon."

"I did not," Morgana said, then snuffled.

Her bottom lip trembled. She threw her head back and bit her lip, but the trembling worsened. So, she threw a fist to her mouth and bit her hand, but by then the tears were cascading down her cheeks. She swiped them away, but they were coming too fast and, with a strangulated screech, she hunched her shoulders and relented from her attempts to be brave. In a seemingly endless torrent, she bawled out a flood of tears as she climbed down from the wagon and held out her arms.

With a bemused glance at Fergal and Randolph, the sheriff also held out his arms and let Morgana fall into them where the crying continued unabated.

"Oh, come on," Fergal said. "You can't believe that performance, can you?"

The sheriff glanced over his rapidly dampening shoulder.

"She's awful unhappy."

"She's not. That's just . . . just . . . just plain pathetic."

"I reckon someone's made this right pretty woman

real sad." The sheriff patted Morgana's back. "So, guess what I'm going to do?"

"You're going to make her give me back my wagon?" Fergal asked, smiling hopefully.

"Nope."

"You're going to make her prove that's her wagon?"

"Nope."

"You're going to make *me* prove that's my wagon."

"Nope. And you've got one last guess before I go and do it anyhow."

Randolph sighed. "You've decided we're the ones who've troubled her and so you're throwing us in jail?"

"Almost right. You trouble her again and I *will* throw you in jail, but I don't want the likes of you littering up my nice clean cells, so I'll just run you out of town."

Randolph glanced down the road at the moth-eaten bay, whose bow legs and bowed back, if anything, bowed even more as he looked at it.

"All right," he said, "but for the sake of our old horse, could you walk us out of town?"

Chapter Three

When Marshal Jim Broughton saw the buzzards circling over the brow of the next hill, he hurried his horse to a fast trot.

He and Deputy Lloyd Henderson had followed Van Romalli's presumed direction for a day. Although they were now ten miles out of Harvest Pass, they were no nearer to finding an outlaw whose ability to disguise himself then melt into nowhere had defeated them for the last six months. In fact, so skilled was his ability to befuddle his victims that they still didn't have a reliable description of him.

Jim glanced at Lloyd, but his deputy was already looking around. And when they crested the hill, ahead lay a burnt-out wagon. It lay on its side, the desperate defenders probably having tipped it over, but from the body Jim could already see, the results of that defense were all to clear.

Still, they approached the wagon on a cautious and circuitous route, but that just let them confirm that the circling buzzards were the only living creatures here. A closer inspection confirmed that only one person had died. He was a white-haired man, who lay beside the wagon with several gunshot wounds peppering his chest.

They searched the body for identification, but found nothing, then searched through the slew of belongings that the raiders had strewn all over the site. They still found nothing of interest, but when they righted the wagon, they discovered who this person was.

Across an unburnt length of cloth was: "Dewey Malone's traveling extravaganza of incredible treasures and amazing—" The fire had destroyed the rest, but it was enough for Jim and Lloyd to exchange a knowing glance.

"Van Romalli," they murmured together.

"The main problem with Romalli," Jim said, "is that he always changes his tactics."

"And he's always one step ahead of us," Lloyd said. "And he's always—"

"I don't need to hear the list."

Jim picked up a crate that probably once contained one of Dewey Malone's incredible treasures. Now it just contained several posters depicting a casket, which Malone had used to display something called the treasure of Saint Woody.

"Saint Woody," Lloyd said. "There's a saint called Woody?"

"Apparently."

They paced around, picking up more emptied crates, many of which had once contained Malone's treasures, but Romalli had been thorough and every one was either empty or contained nothing of value.

When they'd completed their tour of the site, Jim gestured to Lloyd to collect the body of Malone so that they could take him to Harvest Pass for a dignified burial. But then he saw scrape marks on the ground and lowered his hand. These marks followed a straight line and when Jim hunkered down beside them, he decided that to make indentations this deep someone had dragged a heavy object along the ground.

He stood to see the markings disappear into a tangle of grass and, as there had been little to look at there, he followed them. Lloyd hurried to join him and the two men paced into the grass. Within fifty paces, they came across a casket, now lying abandoned, but it matched the poster depicting the casket containing the treasure of Saint Woody.

They circled the casket, then closed in. Jim tapped his foot against the side receiving a solid thud, then stepped back. The casket was closed and about six-feet long, three-feet high and three-feet wide. Solid bands of rusting iron covered each edge and the lid was rounded, but the jeweled circles on the lid drew his attention first. There were five in all and each contained twelve jewels.

As he leaned over and fingered the jewels, Lloyd considered the lid, but failed to find a way to open it. Then he put his shoulder to the side of the casket and strained, but succeeded in only pushing it a foot before he had to relent.

"So," he said, "I can see why Romalli abandoned this. It's mighty heavy, but I'd have thought he'd make the effort for these jewels."

Jim stood back and paced to the side so that the low sun covered the jeweled circles.

"I ain't so sure they are jewels. I reckon they're just colored glass." He snorted. "I mean, with all respect to the dead Dewey Malone, do you really reckon a showman like him would own real jewels?"

As Lloyd nodded, Jim looked back through the grass to the wagon and considered the effort it'd take to drag the casket to the wagon, then right it. He shrugged and gestured for Lloyd to leave the casket where it lay, but as his shadow slipped off the casket, the jewels again drew his attention.

He turned and stood over the casket. The chances of them being worth anything were low, but he couldn't help but stare at them. And this time, he saw that around each jewel there was a carving. They might have depicted animals, perhaps people, but they were stylized. And when he placed his cheek to the casket and stared at them, he saw that the shapes were all different, and that the circles projected out from the casket by a half-inch.

He nudged the first circle and discovered that he could turn it to any position. And when he ran his fingers over the five circles, he found that in the center of the central circle, there was a slot, two inches long and wider than a quarter.

"What do you make of this?" he asked.

Lloyd rejoined him and stared at the circles as Jim turned them, then waggled a finger in the slot. With a knowing nod, he nudged Jim aside and peered inside, then rummaged in his pocket. He removed several coins, which he placed over the slot, one at a time.

"I've got an idea," he said.

"If you want to get in there, I'd use a knife."

"I don't reckon that's what you're supposed to use."

Lloyd showed Jim a nickel, then dropped it in the casket. Rattling sounded inside as the nickel rolled around, but when it stopped moving, Jim smiled.

"And what did that prove, other than you just ain't getting that nickel back?"

"It was just a theory. And one I ain't testing again."

Lloyd gathered up his other coins, but as he shuffled them into his hand, a dollar fell from his grasp. It bounced on the casket lid and landed in the central jeweled circle, then, with terrible inevitability, rolled towards the slot. Both men lunged for the coin, but they were too late and it fell into the slot.

Even as they were wincing, a different, deeper sound than the nickel had made echoed within. Then, with a grinding of gears, the jeweled circles turned, each one revolving in an opposite direction to the circle beside it as, inside the casket, the coin rattled back and forth, taking a complex route.

But then inside, the coin rattled to a halt and, with a fateful clunk, the circles stopped moving, although Jim was sure they were in a different position to what they had been in before.

"Now that sure was strange," he said.

"Strange, but not worth a dollar." Lloyd viewed the casket from all angles and ran his fingers over it, searching for a way in. "Unless I can get my dollar back."

"And perhaps that's what you're *not* supposed to do."

Lloyd stood. "That mean you've figured out what's in the casket?"

"Nope."

Lloyd glanced at Jim to find that he was staring at him with a smile tugging at the corners of his mouth.

"Then you've figured out how to catch Romalli?"

"I haven't." Jim winked. "But I've figured out how the casket will catch Romalli."

The town of Harvest Pass nestled in a valley below with the rail track to Jim's right and a lake sandwiched between two low hills to his left.

Jim was riding alongside Dewey Malone's wagon, which he reckoned was just about capable of completing the journey. On the back of the wagon lay the body of Malone and the casket containing the treasure of Saint Woody. Lloyd was driving the wagon with his face set in a sneer, but whether that was because he'd lost a dollar in the casket or because he didn't like Jim's idea, Jim couldn't tell.

Ahead was a rider coming from Harvest Pass. Jim slowed his horse but when a star on the man's chest caught a stray beam of light, he hurried on ahead to meet him.

"What's the trouble?" he hollered as he pulled up.

"I'm Sheriff Johnson of Harvest Pass," the man said, then narrowed his eyes as he considered Jim then the approaching wagon. He raised his eyebrows. "I'd heard that Marshal Jim Broughton would be heading this way."

"Then you've found him. I'm after Van Romalli, but he got to another poor soul before me—Dewey Malone, a showman."

"Then he was his last victim." The sheriff smiled. "Because I've captured Romalli."

Jim's mouth fell open, and he was embarrassed to detect a pang of irritation that someone else had caught his quarry, but he bit it back and raised his hat.

"That sure is good news. Where is he?"

"Back in my jail cell with his henchman."

"We've never proved that Romalli has an accomplice."

"Then I've done the proving for you."

As Lloyd pulled the rickety wagon to a halt beside him, Jim decided that getting to town and seeing Romalli behind bars was more important than a slow journey into town. He ordered Lloyd to carry on into town on his own, then hurried on with the sheriff toward Harvest Pass.

"How did you capture him?" he asked.

"Didn't know it was him at first. But a traveler arrived in town and told me she'd seen someone who matched Romalli's description chasing after this showman—Dewey Malone, I guess."

"But we have no description of what Romalli looks like."

The sheriff shrugged. "Then the description matched. Anyhow, I figured that Romalli is now targeting showmen. Then he rode into town, bold and brazen as you like, and harasses this poor woman, trying to steal her property. I ran him out of town, but he and his henchman rode back into town and tried again. But I was waiting for him."

"That don't sound like Romalli's tactics."

"I've heard he changes his methods all the time."

"I'd heard that too," Jim murmured, then returned to quiet, preferring to wait until he'd seen Romalli for himself before he voiced any more concerns.

When they arrived in town, they dismounted outside the sheriff's office and Jim waited for the sheriff to head into the office first. On the boardwalk, he mouthed a silent prayer. Then he crossed his fingers, mouthed another prayer, and strode into the office.

Ten seconds later, he was on the boardwalk again, staring out of town and waiting for Lloyd. He hadn't even stayed to make eye contact with the prisoners, he was so sure of himself.

Sheriff Johnson had followed him out and was babbling continuously, but Jim didn't trust himself to speak.

When Lloyd rode into town, he paced off the boardwalk to face his oncoming deputy. He shook his head, Lloyd lowering his for a moment.

"You trying to tell me," Sheriff Johnson said as Lloyd halted the wagon, "that that ain't Van Romalli?"

Still Jim ignored him, and when Lloyd jumped down from the wagon, he directed Lloyd away from the office.

"Romalli's still at large," he said.

"Not even a chance the prisoners could be connected to him?" Lloyd said with a glance at Johnson.

"Nope."

"But they are," Johnson bleated.

Only now that Lloyd had joined him did Jim reckon that he could keep his temper long enough to face the sheriff.

"I've seldom seen anyone who looks less like an outlaw than those two men in there."

"But you've never seen Romalli, so how can you be so sure?"

"I'm a lawman, and I trust my instincts."

"And so do I."

"And what *instincts* made you think you'd got Van Romalli?"

"They lied about everything. They claimed they were tonic sellers, who display authentic historical stuff, and that this pretty young woman had stolen their show. Then they tried to—"

Jim raised a hand, silencing him. "And did it occur to you that maybe that was the truth?"

"Nope."

Jim sighed and waved his hand in a dismissive gesture.

"Just let them go."

"You can't order me around," Johnson grunted, setting his hands on his hips. "This is my town and my—"

"Yeah, yeah. Then don't let them go, but whatever you do, neither of them have anything to do with Van Romalli."

As Johnson wandered into his office, muttering to himself, Lloyd considered the wagon.

"So," he said, "once we've buried Dewey Malone, what are we going to do next?"

"We carry on chasing after . . ." Jim glanced at the office, then at the wagon and at the casket that he could see poking through the cloth. Like the grinding gears that controlled the jeweled circles on the casket lid, Jim felt another cog in his mind slip into place to provide him with the final part of his plan to use the casket to catch Romalli. "We stay in Harvest Pass. I'm tired of chasing after Romalli."

"Me, too, but we have to."

"We don't have to do nothing." Jim patted Lloyd's back and grinned. "Perhaps it's time for Romalli to chase after us."

"We tried to trap him in White Springs and failed. I can't see why that casket will catch him now when he's already abandoned it once before."

"We just need to make sure it's enticing enough for an outlaw like Romalli to try to steal it. And we just need to be close when he does to capture him."

Lloyd shook his head. "I can't see us making that casket enticing whatever we do."

"We couldn't." Jim pointed to the sheriff's office where Johnson was booting two men through the door. One man was thin and wearing a bright green waistcoat. The other man was stocky. "But I know two people who can do it for us."

Chapter Four

A mile out of Harvest Pass, Randolph and Fergal slumped beside the trail.

Today had not been a good day. Not only had they lost everything they owned, been arrested, been run out of town—twice—but now they seriously doubted they'd be able to go anywhere.

The horse Morgana had left them with had finally dug its heels in and refused to go any farther, and was munching grass beside the trail. Even if they could encourage it to move, they doubted it would have the strength to get them to another town. And returning to Harvest Pass for a third time was out of the question.

Their only choice was to wait nearby until Morgana left town and hope they could find a way to reclaim their property.

40

With typical optimism, Fergal had pulled the cloth from the buckboard to make an awning, then removed a rotten plank from the sideboards and placed it over the water barrel. On the plank, he'd set out his dozen remaining bottles of tonic, hoping that somebody might pass by who felt unwell, or whom he could convince they felt unwell.

And as the sun dipped below the horizon, the first people they'd seen since leaving jail were heading toward them.

Fergal nudged Randolph and jumped up to stand beside the barrel, but Randolph couldn't muster the enthusiasm and continued sitting.

Fergal turned to the newcomers. "You two men seem troubled. Could it be that you are feeling unwell?"

The two men pulled their wagon to a halt. It was in almost as bad a state as their buckboard was in with wide burn marks marring the cloth.

"It could not," the largest of the men said. As they dismounted, he introduced himself as Jim then introduced his friend Lloyd.

"And I think it probably could," Fergal persisted. "But I can change all that with my universal remedy to cure all ills. Let me tell you a story. Many years ago, a young man—"

Jim raised a hand. "I might like to hear that story, but first, I have a proposition to make to you."

"Always pleased to hear propositions from a

customer." Fergal shook the bottle, causing the amber liquid inside to sparkle, and smiled.

"I suppose I could buy a bottle," Jim said. "How much?"

"One dollar."

"One dollar for that small bottle!"

"Mine is a genuine product. No ailment is so bad, no—"

"I'll buy it." Jim handed over a coin and took the bottle, then passed it to Lloyd, who shrugged then slipped it into his pocket. "Now, let me offer you a chance of a lifetime."

Fergal sighed. "And how much will this chance of a lifetime cost me?"

"Only one hundred dollars, but you will make a thousand, and that's guaranteed."

"Guaranteed," Fergal snorted. "I ain't interested."

Randolph jumped to his feet and slapped a hand on Fergal's shoulder then drew him aside.

"You heard what he's offering," he whispered, "a chance to make a thousand dollars. And maybe then we'll be able to buy back our wagon."

"We'll find a way to get our wagon back without buying it, but ain't it always the way? Whenever you need to make a lot of money fast, someone offers you a way to make it, but it'll only cost you one hundred dollars."

"Still, it must be worth hearing what it is. It could be a genuine offer."

Fergal snorted his disbelief but when Randolph provided an encouraging smile, he mustered a nod and, to Jim's directions, they trooped around the men's wagon to stand at the back.

With a flourish, Jim pulled back the cloth to reveal a casket.

"Here is your chance of a lifetime," he announced.

Fergal peered at the casket, then fingered the jeweled circles on the lid. He shrugged.

"It's a box," he murmured.

"It is not just a box. I obtained this casket from the great showman, Dewey Malone. It contains the treasure of Saint Woody."

"There's a saint called Woody?"

"There was. And he was a great man. Tell him the story, Lloyd."

"What story?" Lloyd asked.

"The story of Saint Woody and how he found his treasure."

"There's a story?" Lloyd considered Jim, who nudged him in the stomach. "Of course there's a story. Well, let me see now. Yes, the story . . ." Lloyd coughed, then stared aloft with his brow furrowed. Then he smiled. "Once upon a time there was a man called Saint Woody—"

"Although back in those days," Jim said, interrupting, "he was just called Woody."

"Of course, and one day, Woody was . . . was doing something or other, such as . . ."

". . . such as tending his sheep," Jim said, his cheeks reddening by the moment, "and then something happened to change his shepherding life forever when . . . when . . ."

". . . when a great light shone down on him," Lloyd said, a bead of moisture breaking out on his brow, "and he . . ."

". . . and he . . ."

". . . and he had a vision of . . ."

". . . of somebody or other, who told him to . . ."

". . . told him to go somewhere such as . . . the mountains?"

"Yes, he did," Jim said, patting Lloyd's back, "and when Woody got there, after an epic journey, he . . ."

"He found this"—Lloyd gestured to the casket—"he found this here casket and the wondrous treasure that was within. And . . ."

"And some say the treasure is"—Jim clicked his fingers—"it's the keys to heaven itself and legend has it that . . ."

"Legend has it . . ."

"Legend has . . ."

Jim and Lloyd bowed their heads.

"Legend . . ."

"Leg . . ."

"Thank you for that most inspiring story, gentleman," Fergal said, putting the embarrassed storytellers out of their misery. "Your eloquence has sure convinced me that the treasure of Saint Woody is genuine. So, show me the treasure."

"I cannot," Jim said, regaining his composure with a shrug of his jacket, "and there lies the beauty of the casket. To see the treasure, you must give me a dollar."

Fergal fingered the sum total of his wealth, then shook his head.

"Use your own dollar."

Jim sighed but then turned the circles on the casket lid to a new position. He gestured for Lloyd to give him a dollar and, after both men had exchanged a glare, fed it into the hole in the casket lid.

Inside the casket, gears ground, the circles turned, and the dollar rolled around, the sound far louder than Randolph would have expected. It traversed the length of the casket, then back, then followed a complex path that took in all corners of the casket, and even sounded as if it rose back up to the top again.

But then the coin clattered to a halt and all was silent.

"And the treasure?" Fergal asked.

"Sadly, there is no sight of the treasure this time."

Fergal tipped back his hat. "And sticking a dollar in a box, which rattles, then watching five glass circles go round and round will make me a thousand dollars, will it?"

"Guaranteed."

Fergal paced around the wagon considering the casket from all angles.

"The idea is that there are hundreds of possible patterns of symbols, but only one pattern will open the box. So, you turn the circles, put your dollar in, and hope you're lucky enough to pick the one pattern that will open the box and get you to the treasure of this great man, Saint Woody."

Jim grinned. He glanced back at Lloyd, who also grinned.

"I can see I have come to the right man. You have deduced the casket's potential correctly."

"And you're selling this superb opportunity that will make its owner a thousand dollars, guaranteed, for one hundred dollars?"

"I am."

"Then I have to ask the obvious question. If this really is a chance of a lifetime, why sell it?"

"It is a long and terrible story. But I will tell it to you if you wish."

"Not another story," Lloyd murmured.

Fergal glanced at Lloyd. "To spare your friend the indignity, I do not. But I assume that whatever terrible story you will torture me with, the truth is that when Dewey Malone sold it to you, he *forgot* to tell you which combination of symbols will open the box. And now you can't get into it every night to take out the money everybody has put into it during the day and, without that information, the box is utterly worthless."

"You are a perceptive man."

"And furthermore, I'd suggest that the treasure of Saint Woody is not just a very bad story. But that it is also a self-fulfilling story because the actual treasure is the money people put into the box when they try to claim that treasure."

"You continue to amaze me with your understanding."

Fergal rubbed his chin, then patted the lid. "And you've tried all the combinations you can think of?"

"Yeah."

"You tried blasting it open?" Randolph asked.

"Everything."

Fergal nodded. "Then I'll buy it."

"Fergal," Randolph urged, but Fergal was smiling.

"I will give you the sum total of my wealth in all the world."

"Which is?" Jim asked.

"One dollar." Fergal waved the dollar Jim had given him.

"That isn't enough."

Fergal gestured back at his display of tonic bottles.

"Then buy more bottles of my tonic and I will raise my offer."

"I am no fool."

"Then try this—if I can find a way to open the box and make more than one hundred dollars in the next week, I'll buy it. If not, I'll return the casket to you." Fergal smiled. "You can trust me."

Jim and Lloyd backed away and exchanged a short conversation.

Randolph also drew Fergal back.

"I reckon," Randolph said, "that they'd prefer that one hundred dollars now."

"I reckon so, too, but one dollar is the best we can offer right now."

Jim returned and held out a hand.

"Deal," he said. "And I reckon you're the kind of man who'll get everything he deserves from that casket."

Fergal considered Jim's and Lloyd's fixed smiles, then shrugged and shook the hand.

"I can't believe you bought this," Randolph said, when Jim and Lloyd had left them.

"But," Fergal said, patting the casket, "there could already be huge amounts of money in here."

Randolph sat on the back of the buckboard beside the casket and considered it.

"If there is money in it, my guess is that it's only that one dollar Jim put in it."

"That's possible, but I also reckon I was right and Jim didn't know how to get the best use out of this box."

"That's obvious. But I don't reckon we can open it either."

"Perhaps we don't have to." Fergal threw Randolph his only dollar. "Put that in it."

"That's our last dollar. I'm not losing it in the box."

"Trust me."

Randolph stared at Fergal, but on seeing that smile he'd seen so often, he stood, then thought lucky thoughts. He turned the circles on the lid to a new position, then fed the dollar into the casket.

The circles turned and the coin rattled as it rolled around, taking a route that Randolph was sure was different to before, but after nearly a minute of rattling, the coin stopped and the circles clunked to a halt.

But the casket remained closed.

"And what did that prove?" Randolph grumbled. "Aside from the fact that we ain't got no money now."

"It proved how we can rebuild our fortunes with this box."

Fergal rolled beneath the buckboard and rummaged in the dirt, then stood. He favored Randolph with a conspiratory wink, then handed the dollar back to him. Then he winked again and gave him another dollar.

"How did you do that?" Randolph said, raising his eyebrows with genuine surprise.

Fergal beckoned Randolph to join him in crawling beneath the buckboard. They lay on their backs and stared through the gaps in the buckboard bottom at the underside of the casket. And, from this position, Randolph saw another slot in the center of the casket's base.

"They *were* using it wrong," Fergal said. "The box doesn't eat your money. It just rattles around inside and makes the circles turn. And all those spinning jewels stop you from noticing that when the coin stops, the box spits it out of the bottom."

"You're right," Randolph said, rolling out from under the buckboard. "But how will a box with a hole in the top and another hole in the bottom make us rich?"

"Only question is," Fergal said, raising a finger as he emerged from beneath the buckboard, "how can it do anything other than make us rich?"

Chapter Five

An hour after sunup, Randolph pulled the buckboard up on the outskirts of Harvest Pass, but at the
opposite end to Morgana Sullivan.

After Sheriff Johnson had twice run them out of
town the previous day, he reckoned they were pushing their luck in thinking that staying right on the
edge of town would technically still qualify as being
out of town. But as long as they made no effort to approach Morgana, he reckoned they stood a chance of
the sheriff letting them stay.

Randolph threw back the cloth from the back of
the buckboard, then placed the small podium he'd
made last night on the ground, while Fergal stood on
the seat ready to return to doing what he was best at.

And when the first man they'd seen today wandered

toward the stable, Fergal threw his thin arms wide to reveal his bright green waistcoat.

"Roll up, roll up," he announced. "You are the first person today to receive the chance of a lifetime."

The man continued to pace toward the stable, but then did a double-take on realizing that Fergal was hailing him and turned.

"What chance of a lifetime?" he asked.

"A chance to win the treasure of Saint Woody."

"There's a saint called Woody?"

"You mean you haven't heard of him?" Fergal glared down at the man, defying him to doubt such a person existed, then watched the man shake his head. "Then do you have time to hear a wondrous tale about this most sainted of men?"

"I ain't got the time." The man turned to the stable. "I've got my horse to collect."

"Many years ago," Fergal announced, apparently not hearing the man and definitely not giving him a chance to escape, "a young man by the name of Woody was tending his flock of sheep. He was bored because he didn't want to be a sheepherder all his life and he dreamt of achieving great things. Perhaps a little like you and I."

"Yeah," the man said, not looking back, but he stopped in the stable doorway, then turned and shuffled closer to the buckboard. "What happened to this Woody?"

"It was a most wondrous thing. The clouds parted

and there was a clap of thunder and a vision came to Woody of a bewitching woman. She glowed from head to foot and had a face that shone with divine wisdom. And she enticed Woody to join her in her mountain lair." Fergal winked, receiving another shuffled pace closer in return. "So, he left his sheep and trudged ever higher into the hills. After many days, he reached the top of a craggy mountain where the snow lay crisply on the ground and the air was so thin he had to gasp. There, he found a fabulous jeweled casket and in that casket was the most stupendous treasure in all the world."

The man shuffled another pace closer to the buckboard.

"What was it?"

"I don't know, because the bewitching woman appeared to him again and beckoned Woody to come closer and, just as he reached for the treasure, she closed the lid of the fabulous casket. And it has never been opened since."

The man peered around Fergal to see the side of the casket on the back of the buckboard.

"And that's the fabulous jeweled casket, is it?"

"It sure is."

The man paced around the side of the buckboard, nodding, then stopped beside the casket. He swiped a finger along its side then considered the grime he'd collected.

"Perhaps you should buy a bottle of Morgana's

universal cleaner, then it might look a bit more fabulous."

Fergal gritted his teeth. "The grime is hard-earned and a sign of the authenticity of this most wondrous of treasures."

"Morgana's got an authentic fragment from *The Mayflower*," the man said, folding his arms. "Now that's authentic. And it's clean."

"If that fragment from *The Mayflower* is so authentic, why is it the same color as her wagon?"

"I don't know. I hadn't thought of that."

Fergal didn't mention that he knew this because he had painted that particular piece of authentic memorabilia himself, but he did jump down from the buckboard to place a friendly hand on the man's back. With a gentle nudge, he directed him toward the podium at the back of the buckboard.

"And you can only *look* at Morgana's exhibits," he said as they both climbed on to the podium to look down at the casket. "But this casket is different. You can do so much more."

"Like what?"

Fergal patted the jeweled circles. "Well, the bewitching woman asked Woody to place these jewels—"

"They look like colored glass to me. I really think you should get a bottle of Morgana's cleaner."

"Not everything that shines is expensive, and often the dullest of objects are the most precious."

"I still prefer shiny objects."

"You may," Fergal persisted, "but the woman asked Woody to place these symbols in an order that told the story of his life, proclaiming that only that order would open the casket. Woody did this, but the woman so entranced him that he forsook the treasure within and left the mountain lair with her to roam the world, spreading his message of peace and of the denial of material possessions. And when his family came looking for him, all they found was this casket and, when they tried to open it, they could not."

The man nodded. "Because they did not know the story of Woody's life?"

"Exactly. Only Woody knew his own story, but if anyone should ever deduce it, they can turn the circles to tell that story and they will be the only person other than Saint Woody to see the treasure."

"And what do you reckon this treasure is?"

"Who is to say?" Fergal leaned to the man and cupped a hand over his ear. "Although I have heard it said that the treasure could even be the keys to heaven itself."

"Seeing something like that would be nice."

Fergal patted the man's back. "And for just a dollar, you get a chance to open the casket, and if it does open, you also get to keep the treasure within."

The man rubbed his hands. "It'll only cost a dollar to get a fabulous treasure like the keys to heaven itself?"

"Just one dollar."

"And how many goes do I get?"

Fergal grinned. "As many as you need."

With sundown approaching, Fergal's and Randolph's fortunes had changed.

Earlier in the day, when Fergal wasn't looking, Randolph had used a bottle of universal remedy to buff up the casket and the shining casket instantly became even more enticing than before. And, for the rest of the day, a stream of customers had wandered out of town to try their luck at winning the treasure of Saint Woody.

Some customers needed Fergal's version of the tale of Saint Woody to encourage them to try their luck, but most realized that if money went into the casket, the person who opened it would claim that money, no matter how uninteresting the treasure of Saint Woody proved to be.

What these people didn't see was the sand box that Randolph had constructed beneath the buckboard to silently collect the coins when they emerged from the slot in the bottom of the casket.

With no idea that they were vying to win what was probably an empty casket, enthusiasm was great. Throughout the day, customers applied all manner of methods to winning, from kicking the casket, to cursing the casket, and even praying to the casket, but all methods failed and the casket remained resolutely closed.

And the sand box beneath the casket grew in weight.

When Randolph checked during a rare quiet time, they were already closing on the one hundred dollars they needed to buy the casket outright. And if they could continue their good fortune, it'd only be a matter of days before they'd be in a more prosperous position than the state they had been in when Morgana stole their wagon.

Sheriff Johnson did wander down the road to see them, but such was the good-natured enthusiasm of the crowd which was queuing to try its luck that his only response was to try himself, without success.

But just as they'd decided that no more customers would try their luck today, a man rode into town and pulled up beside them. He wore large round spectacles that made his eyes appear as if they were twice their size, and his eight-horse team was dragging the longest wagon Randolph had ever seen. It appeared to have been constructed from hitching together four covered wagons and the whole train flexed back and forth as he dragged his horses to a halt.

"I believe I'm looking for you," he said, tipping his hat to Fergal.

"Then I'm most pleased to meet you," Fergal said, his tone cautious. "But I don't give refunds. I'm sure that whatever ailment I said my tonic would cure will go away if you give it another week."

"I have never bought a tonic from you."

"Then I'm even more pleased to meet you." Fergal frowned. "But why are you looking for me?"

"I've heard that you are the owner of the greatest show on all the Earth."

Fergal glanced over his shoulder at his moldering buckboard and his equally moldering horse, then shrugged.

"Some have claimed as such."

"Then I have found the right man." He jumped down from his wagon. "My name is Milton Moon and you and I are about to become good friends."

Fergal reached up and patted the casket. "And would my good friend like to invest a dollar to try to claim the treasure of Saint Woody?"

"There's a saint called Woody?"

"There sure is."

Milton furrowed his brow, but then shrugged and climbed on to the podium.

"And the treasure is in here?" he asked, pointing at the casket.

"It sure is. You choose a position for the jewels, then insert a dollar in this slot, and—"

"Ah, yes, I see." Milton tapped the circles while nodding so vigorously his glasses bounced on his nose. "Twelve symbols on five different circles. Assuming that all combinations are possible and that they are all equally likely that would mean . . ." Milton closed his eyes as he flexed his fingers back and forth, mouthing numbers.

"Just hundreds of possible combinations, but if you find the correct one, the casket will present you with the treasure of Saint Woody. And it is fabulous. Some say that the treasure is the keys to—"

"Two hundred and forty-eight thousand eight hundred and thirty-two combinations to be exact," Milton said, beaming proudly. "And then assuming that to crack the code you must both find the correct opening configuration and the closing configuration. And that the former does not determine the latter, that means . . ."

Fergal smiled as Milton's eyes glazed.

"Several hundred more possible combinations?"

"You could say that. I will not belabor you with the exact number. Suffice to say it is a very large number indeed, but I believe that statistics won't help the person who risks a dollar on this foolhardy venture."

"And you are right. The successful investor must deduce the story of Saint Woody's life."

Milton eyed the casket from a variety of angles, then nodded.

"Or be an expert in the art of mathematical manipulation." Milton rocked his head from side to side, then slapped a fist in his palm. "Ah, yes, I see how it works. Very ingenious."

Fergal considered Milton's smile, then leaned toward him.

"Which is?"

Milton shrugged. "But it is your casket. Surely you know how to open it."

"I do," Fergal muttered through gritted teeth. "I just want to know if you know."

"But I do."

Fergal set his determined gaze on Milton, who returned that gaze, but when Milton was the first to break eye contact, he smiled and pointed to the slot.

"Then put a dollar in the casket and prove it."

"I could, but I reckon I wouldn't like what I'd find inside, but that is not the reason I've come to see you. I have a proposition for you."

Fergal sighed. "And I guess this proposition is a chance of a lifetime?"

"How did you guess?"

"I just know. And I also guess that this chance of a lifetime will make me a thousand dollars in a matter of days, guaranteed."

"Perhaps ten times that in a matter of hours, and all in return for sponsoring me with just a few dollars."

Fergal paced down from the podium. "How few?"

"After my long journey, I have some breakages and need the services of a blacksmith, and I need the use of two strong men, but that's all."

Fergal blew out his cheeks, but then nodded, and beckoned Randolph to join them.

As they flashed skeptical glances at each other, Milton walked them to the back of his train of wagons, then threw back the cover. Fergal peered at the huge piles of material within.

"It's a pile of cloth," he murmured.

"Actually, it is the finest silk, but it is not just any pile of silk."

"And I guess this was the silk that the Pilgrim Fathers wove on their first day in the New World, or . . ."

"Or," Randolph offered, "Columbus used it as a sail when he crossed the Atlantic."

Milton patted Randolph's arm. "You are very close. But this silk will be even more famous than that after I have used it for a very different maiden voyage."

"From where?" Fergal asked. "And to where?"

"From that hill over there." Milton pointed to the hill that overlooked the lake to the east of town, then drew Fergal round to point to the hill on the opposite side of the lake about a quarter-mile away. "To that hill over there!"

"I'm impressed," Fergal intoned, forcing as much sarcasm as he could into his tone.

"You should be. People will pay thousands of dollars to see it."

Fergal glanced at the pile of silk, then turned to look at the hills and the lake, then back to consider the silk again. He shook his head, then draped a friendly arm around Milton's neck and drew him closer.

"Milton, I pride myself on being able to see the potential in a whole lot of the wildest money-making schemes there have ever been. But no matter how enthusiastic you are, I don't reckon anybody will pay to see you and that heap of silk head from that hill over there to that hill over there."

"But they will because . . ." Milton shrugged away from Fergal. "Ah, did I not mention one small detail?"

"You did miss out the bit where you explained why going from that hill over there to that hill over there will make me thousands of dollars."

"Perhaps I did. Well, it works like this. I will be going from that hill over there to that hill over there in a straight line."

Fergal snorted. "It still don't excite me."

"It is a very straight line."

"It could be the straightest line there ever has been and nobody will pay to see you do it."

"They will. Because I will go from that hill over there to that hill over there in a line that is so straight, I won't even touch the ground." Milton slapped the silk. "This is my flying wagon."

"Your *flying* wagon?" Fergal and Randolph said together.

"You got it. My wagon will sail serenely through

the air between the hills without anything to connect it to the ground. And people will pay to see that."

Fergal rubbed his chin. A slow grin emerged.

"And they would. The only question is—just how quickly can you get out of town before they realize your flying wagon won't get off the ground?"

Milton snapped his head back. "This is not a scheme to cheat people out of their money. Mine is a genuine invention."

"Of course it is, and if you say it loud enough you can even convince yourself."

"You do it all the time," Randolph murmured.

"But we still have to work out how we can escape quickly, just in case this *flying* wagon's wings don't flap hard enough."

"My flying wagon does not have wings." Milton stood back. "And I had heard that a great showman was coming to Harvest Pass, not some . . . some . . . some cheap huckster."

"I am not a—" Fergal narrowed his eyes. "Where did you hear that a great showman was coming to Harvest Pass?"

"I saw the posters. The greatest show on all the Earth, they said. Coming to Harvest Pass to amaze, they said. They never said that the greatest show on all the Earth would be you, your grinning friend, a half-dead horse, and a puzzle box I could have solved as a child."

"Now listen here," Randolph muttered, jabbing a firm finger against Milton's chest. But before he could vent his feelings, a trumpet call blasted down the road, stunning all three men into silence.

They turned to look, as did every other person who was outside.

At the other end of the road, a rider was galloping into town while playing a rallying call with all his might. He wore a white costume that was so bright it glowed in the sunlight, and a white hat sprinkled with silver that glowed even brighter. And when he drew his horse to a halt and paused for breath, the dazzling smile he provided was nearly bright enough to induce temporary blindness.

When he restarted his trumpet call, two other riders hurtled by him, both decked out in white costumes and spinning lariats above their heads. These riders circled around the edges of the road, one on each side and traveling in opposite directions, galloping by the buildings so close that people had to leap on to the boardwalk to avoid them. And if anyone had been leaning on the hitching rail, they could have touched them as they passed.

But their sure-footed mounts missed everyone and the lariat twirlers didn't miss a beat as they swirled their ropes over their heads, down their bodies then up again.

Then two more white-clad riders surged past the trumpet player and followed them down the road.

These riders were not spinning lariats, but they were standing on their horses. They also hurtled round the edge of the buildings and now that the townsfolk's original shock had receded, everyone began a steady handclap and encouraged the people who had been inside to come outside and watch the show.

When the riders were circling on their third pass of the main road, cheering people thronged the board-walks and the occasional good-natured gunshot ripped into the air.

Then two more riders galloped past the trumpet player, and just to beat the other two sets of perform-ers, these were both standing on their horses *and* spinning lariats.

Round and round the riders surged, their circles becoming smaller and smaller until they formed a continuous line around the trumpet player.

But then, with a sudden coordinated movement, everyone drew their horses to a halt and spun their mounts to face outwards. The riders jumped down, tumbling over their shoulders before coming up with their hands held high.

As they knelt, applause ripped out from all corners of the road, but the trumpet player silenced it with a final loud rally. Then he gestured and his trumpet disappeared in a puff of smoke.

Even as the townsfolk's gasps were still echoing, he burst out of the circle of horses and rode at break-neck speed down the center of the road. Then he dragged his horse around with reckless speed and pulled it to a halt outside the saloon where he faced the bulk of the crowd.

The horse reared, but he recovered so quickly that this was probably planned. Then he walked the horse in a circle with its front legs held high, before bringing it to a halt directed toward the saloon.

The horse knelt, bending its forelegs to let the rider walk off on to the ground. Then he stood before his horse, his legs planted wide, his square jaw held high, the sun gleaming off his pristine teeth and bright eyes.

Then he whipped out a huge scroll from his jacket and gestured for quiet from all corners of the road.

A round of hushing from the crowd gave him the silence he requested within seconds.

"Citizens of Harvest Pass," he boomed, "I am Ezekiel T Montgomery and I invite you all to my Wild West show where the greatest showman alive will present to you the greatest show on all the Earth."

Then the performers jumped to their feet and scattered. Posters that appeared as if from nowhere came to hand, and they hurried along the boardwalks handing them out to the eager hands. And as they passed, a wave of desperate people crowded around the ones who had been lucky enough to grab a poster so that they could discover what this Wild West show was all about.

At the end of the road, Randolph, Fergal and Milton stood with their mouths hanging open, transfixed.

Milton was the first to snap out of his trance.

"Ah," he said, "I believe Ezekiel T Montgomery was the man I wanted to see."

Chapter Six

The greatest show on all the Earth was in town.

The prime rule of shows is that when the greatest show on all the Earth is in town, a show that is only the second best in town will receive little custom. And a show that is only the second best on the road is looking at a very quiet time indeed.

Ezekiel T Montgomery had fenced off an area on the outskirts of Harvest Pass inside which were a circle of stalls. Inside that circle, there was Milton Moon's wagon, a tent where Ezekiel and his troupe stayed, and a corral in which they provided the main entertainment.

Fergal and Randolph hadn't bothered to get close enough to see what that entertainment was, but from the crowds of expectant people who went to see it and the smiling faces they sported when they returned, they deduced that these people were getting value for their money.

As for the lawmen Jim and Lloyd, having laid their trap by giving Fergal and Randolph something that was sure to attract Romalli's attention, they could do nothing but wait for their plans to come to fruition. So they kept a close eye on Fergal's and Randolph's activities, while staying out of their sight. Although the arrival of the greatest show on all the Earth made them wonder whether they'd picked the right people to watch because the treasure of Saint Woody appeared to have permanently lost its appeal.

After a long day in which nobody had invested a dollar to win the treasure, Fergal and Randolph were spending as much time glaring down the road at Morgana as they were at trying to entice new customers.

But, as the sun set on an unsuccessful day, Morgana headed toward them.

Randolph alerted Fergal and the two men busied themselves with appearing industrious by rummaging in the back of the buckboard, then jumping up and flinching back as if they were surprised to see her.

"Getting much custom?" she asked.

"Enough to satisfy us," Fergal said, jumping to the ground.

"Then you must have low ambitions."

Fergal grunted and took a long pace toward her but Randolph held him back.

"Don't let her rile you," he whispered.

"She already has," Fergal grunted, struggling but failing to break Randolph's grip.

"But Ezekiel's reduced her custom, too, and before long, she'll have to move on. And when she hasn't got Sheriff Johnson's protection, we can have this discussion again."

Fergal considered Morgana and the sweet smile she was providing, then gave a knowing nod and, with a pat on the back, Randolph released him.

"I do have high ambitions," he said, straightening his jacket, "unlike you, who just settles for stealing off men like me."

"I have ambitions too."

Fergal glanced over his shoulder at Ezekiel's show.

"Then why ruin our lives? Why not pick on a showman like him?"

"Because I enjoy stealing from people like you." Morgana winked and turned away, but then turned back and faced Randolph. "Oh, and Randolph, don't go thinking I'll leave town any time soon so you can bushwhack me on the trail and steal back your wagon. Despite Ezekiel, I'm still selling enough cleaner here to earn me a living for years."

She giggled then sauntered down the road, swinging her skirts and whistling.

"She's right," Fergal muttered. "She can wait us out longer than we can wait her out."

Randolph leaned back against the buckboard.

"But you're right too. I don't see why she picked on us and not on a big showman like Ezekiel T Montgomery."

"Because he's just too big and because . . ." Fergal rubbed his chin as he watched Morgana jump back on to the wagon at the end of the road. "But maybe she was lying, and maybe she is looking to steal from Ezekiel."

"What makes you think that?"

"I don't." Fergal smiled as Randolph furrowed his brow, but then pointed across the road. "And stop looking so confused. I reckon it's time we spent an evening in the saloon, asking questions and hearing some answers."

"Sounds good to me." Randolph narrowed his eyes. "And then what?"

"And then you're going to see Ezekiel."

"I doubt he'll want to see me."

Fergal chuckled. "Even better."

Randolph and Fergal spent the evening in the Lucky Star, questioning anyone who was keen to talk about Ezekiel T Montgomery's show, but everybody reckoned his show really was the greatest show on all the Earth. It had everything: Daredevil riding on horseback, precision shooting, precision shooting on horseback, wild mustang riding, precision shooting while riding a wild mustang . . .

They didn't stay to hear just how wide the attractions were, but they learnt enough about the layout of Ezekiel's compound to satisfy them.

Then they left the saloon and split up. Fergal paced down the road toward his former wagon, while Randolph wandered to the outskirts of town to peer at Ezekiel's show from a safe distance. The last performance had been some hours ago and it was now quiet, but Ezekiel's two main performers, Buck Albright and Hodge Williams were on guard at the gates.

Whistling a nonchalant tune, Randolph wandered closer, and Buck and Hodge paced out to stand before him.

"Next show is tomorrow," Buck said, smiling.

"I know," Randolph said, "but I'd like to see Ezekiel."

"Ezekiel is a busy man. And he doesn't need to talk to everyone that wants to talk to him."

"I'm a fellow showman." Randolph pointed into town. "Me and Fergal show our—"

"So," Hodge said, "you're the pathetic owners of that treasure of Saint Woody, are you?"

"We are."

Buck sneered. "Didn't know there was a saint called Woody."

"Well, there is, and we have his treasure."

"In that case, you definitely ain't seeing Ezekiel."

"But I'd like to discuss how we can come to an agreement to avoid us being in competition."

"You ain't in competition with nobody. But you are going away."

Buck twirled his fingers round then pointed, indicating that Randolph should head back to where he had come from and, unable to think of a way to prolong this conversation, Randolph headed back into town.

The gazes of both men burned the back of his neck and he heard footfalls as they followed him, but he didn't look back. But, on the edge of town, he stopped and lifted a foot to the boardwalk, then bent to bat imaginary dust from his boot.

In the quiet, he listened to the footfalls approaching from behind. Then the paces quickened. He swirled round to confront them, but he was too slow and both men slammed into him.

Randolph danced back, avoiding being bundled on to his back, but he tripped over the side of the boardwalk and wheeled backwards. Before he righted himself, Buck's solid blow to the jaw flattened him to the wall, a follow through jab to the stomach bent him double, and a round-armed slug under the chin cracked his head back against the wall.

His vision whirled. He drew in a great gasp of air, then whirled his fists, throwing punches blind. The first two missed, but the third connected with someone's cheek and, with his vision returned, he stormed in, flailing his fists.

He got in two solid blows to Buck's jaw, and a third blow wheeled him over the hitching rail for him to do a complete circle before slamming down on his back. Randolph batted his hands together as he watched Buck flounder, but before he had time to look for Hodge rough hands grabbed him from behind and dragged him up close.

Randolph thrust his heel back, aiming to stamp on Hodge's foot, but his opponent had his feet set in a wide stance and held Randolph's arms in a firm grip. With no choice, Randolph could do nothing but walk backwards as Hodge dragged him into the alley beside the saloon.

In the dark, Buck rolled to his feet and walked toward him, gradually straightening, with a gleam in his eye that said Randolph was about to regret knocking him over.

"What's this about?" Randolph said, raising his chin and meeting Buck's gaze.

"Mr. Montgomery don't like rivals. And what Mr. Montgomery don't like, we don't like."

"We aren't Ezekiel's rivals. You've already said that."

Buck cracked his knuckles and drew back his fist to its utmost.

"You ain't rivals for nobody, but any dollar the likes of you earn is another dollar that Mr. Montgomery don't earn." Buck glanced at his fist. "Now, you've got yourself a choice, get out of town, or—"

"Or what?"

"Or get a beating and then get out of town."

"We aren't leaving town."

"That wasn't one of the choices."

Buck advanced on Randolph, who went limp in Hodge's grip hoping to give himself leverage to throw him aside, but then two shadows fell across the edge of the alley. Randolph looked toward them and, with Hodge also nudging to the side to look, Buck lowered his fist and glanced over his shoulder.

Jim and Lloyd strode into the end of the alley.

"What's happening here?" Jim asked, peering into the gloom of the alley.

"Nothing but a friendly chat," Buck said, flashing a grin. "Ain't that so, Randolph?"

"Yeah," Randolph said and, as Hodge slackened his grip, elbowed him away. "Nothing but a friendly chat going on here."

"Then you won't mind if we have our own friendly chat with Randolph now, will you?"

"I guess not." Buck turned to the end of the alley, then turned back and tipped his hat with mock politeness. "But if you're still around later, Randolph, we'll have another friendly chat."

"I'll look forward to it," Randolph said, tipping his hat as he aped Buck's surly smile. "If you've got the nerve."

Buck grunted his displeasure at this taunt, then swung back, his fist rising to punch Randolph, but Randolph ducked the blow, then charged him and bundled him back against the wall.

Behind him, Randolph heard Lloyd and Jim dash into the alley then trade blows with Hodge, but Randolph ignored them and concentrated on his fight with Buck.

He pressed him flat against the wall and held him there, signifying with his firm grip that he could better him if he wanted to, but was choosing not to hit him. But Buck didn't take the hint and squirmed out from Randolph's grip then threw another wild punch at him.

Randolph swayed back from the blow, feeling it waft past his nose, then charged in with a flurry of punches. He pummeled Buck one way then the other, then knocked him out on to the boardwalk with a round-armed slug.

Buck skidded over the timbers before coming to a halt, half-on, half-off the boardwalk. He lay a moment, staring at the stars, then shuffled to a sitting position.

Buck glanced to Randolph's side to see that

Hodge was lying on his belly with Lloyd kneeling on his back.

In case Buck chose to escalate this confrontation, Randolph inched his hand toward his holster, but with a sneer Buck raised his hands then swiped his hat from the edge of the alley. This submission encouraged Lloyd to roll off Hodge, then push him out on to the road where he stumbled into Buck.

The two men righted themselves and, with a last arrogant glare at Randolph and the others, strode away toward Ezekiel's show.

Randolph paced out on to the boardwalk to watch them leave, then turned to Jim and Lloyd.

"You fine?" Lloyd asked.

"Yeah," Randolph said, tipping his hat. "And I'm obliged for your help."

"No problem. It is our job."

"Your job?"

"Yeah," Jim said, then glanced at Lloyd and coughed. "We've got our investment to protect."

"Well, you need to think what you want to do about that, because even without their threats, I reckon we'll have to leave town soon. We can't compete with Ezekiel's show, and it'll be even worse when Milton Moon's flying wagon is ready."

Jim looked away, rubbing his chin.

"Does that mean," he said, his voice low, "you're heading out of town and on to the open trail with a box full of money?"

"Yup."

Jim flashed a smile, then turned to go.

"Then I wish you luck." Both men strode away.

"But," Randolph said, halting them, "how will we find you to pay for the casket? I reckon we want to keep it, but we ain't collected one hundred dollars yet."

"Don't worry." Jim looked over his shoulder. "We'll find you."

Randolph watched the two men walk into the saloon. He shrugged then headed down the road.

"Fergal," he said as he jumped on to the back of their buckboard, "you wouldn't believe what's just happened to me."

Fergal stopped fiddling with the circles on the top of the casket to glance at the bruise on Randolph's chin, then at the dirt on his jacket.

"Some of Ezekiel T Montgomery's performers waylaid you, then told you to leave town or else."

"You got it."

Fergal rubbed his hands. "Then everything is going according to plan."

Chapter Seven

At sunup, Morgana's wagon sat at the opposite end of town, seemingly deserted.

Sitting on the front of the buckboard, both men watched the wagon, waiting for Morgana to show herself, but after an hour she still hadn't appeared and, as they were getting twitchy, they walked down the road.

When they reached the wagon it still appeared deserted, and Fergal and Randolph were just debating whether to grab it now and make a run for it when they heard footfalls pacing behind them. They stood tall then continued walking past the wagon, whistling a merry, innocent tune, but from behind them Sheriff Johnson coughed.

"What are you doing?" he asked.

Fergal and Randolph walked on then glanced around, feigning surprise that the sheriff had been addressing them with open mouths and fingers pointing at their chests.

"You mean us?" they said together.

"I do mean you. It looked to me like you were planning to steal your wagon."

"We were doing nothing of the sort," Fergal muttered, his jaw set firm with mock indignation. "We were just—you just said, 'your wagon.'"

Johnson sighed. "I sure did. The wagon *is* yours."

"Well, of course it is, but what made you realize?"

"Because last night Morgana Sullivan broke into Ezekiel T Montgomery's tent and stole his takings before he could bank them."

"And you caught her?"

"Eventually. Someone was seen sneaking away from the tent. I followed the trail and it ended in her . . . your wagon. I found all the evidence I need to convict her." He sighed. "And I guess that's all the proof I need that she did the same to you. You can leave town with your property as soon as you like."

Sheriff Johnson continued talking and may even have offered an apology for arresting them earlier, but neither Randolph nor Fergal heard it. They were too busy dancing a jig.

"I don't like doing this," Randolph said.

Fergal followed Randolph's gaze to see that the

moth-eaten bay was considering them with watery eyes. It stood outside the stable where they had hitched it back on to Morgana's festering buckboard.

"We've got to leave it, Randolph. The speed we sometimes have to travel will probably kill it."

"It ain't just the horse. It's Morgana. She's in a jail cell and that ain't the right place for no woman."

"She's getting what she deserves," Fergal snapped, "just like anybody that does wrong."

"So, if bad things happen to bad people, where does that leave us?"

"We aren't bad."

"But we push the boundaries." Randolph slapped his thigh. "And I reckon that framing her by breaking into Ezekiel's tent and stealing his money, making sure someone saw you, but not too close so that they'd know it wasn't a woman, leaving a trail to the wagon, then—"

"Be quiet, Randolph," Fergal urged. He nudged him then looked up and down the deserted road. "Somebody might hear you."

"And after what you did," Randolph whispered, "perhaps somebody should."

"Quit whining. You were distracting Buck and Hodge while I did it."

"And our other two shadows, Jim and Lloyd." Randolph sighed. "But that just makes me feel even worse about getting Morgana arrested for something she didn't do."

"We just did to her what she did to us." Fergal considered Randolph's frown, then flashed a smile. "And I reckon she really was planning to steal from Ezekiel. I just did my duty as a good citizen and helped out the law."

"You can't twist out of that one, Fergal. That was sneaky even for us."

Fergal sighed long and hard. "What will ease your conscience?"

"We do the right thing, and then good things might happen to us. So, now that we've got back our wagon, we should find a way to get Morgana out of jail."

Fergal tipped back his hat to scratch his forehead and, from the steady rocking of his head, Randolph reckoned he was seriously considering his suggestion.

"Randolph," he said, his voice low and weary, "you're a good man, but I'm setting a limit to that goodness. Morgana got what she deserved, and we're back on the trail."

Randolph searched for something to say to make Fergal change his mind, but in the determined set of his jaw he saw that this was one argument he'd never win.

"And what about our horse?" he asked, fighting for one small victory.

"We've got our horses back."

"I mean the one Morgana left us." Randolph

tapped Fergal's arm and signified that he should look at Morgana's bay, which took that moment to look at them and cock its head on one side. "It'll probably be dead long before she gets out of jail."

"I guess someone will find a use for it."

"Like what?"

"I guess nobody would eat anything that old, but most dogs aren't that choosy and—"

"Fergal!"

Fergal sighed. "All right. If it'll keep you quiet, hitch it to the wagon. But if it slows us down, we will leave it."

Randolph patted Fergal's back, then jumped down from the wagon to secure the horse.

Two minutes later, they trundled out of town and, as if Fergal's suggested fate for slow horses had encouraged the bow-legged bay, they achieved a fair pace.

They swung round so that they'd pass Ezekiel's show. Milton Moon's long line of wagons had been unloaded, which suggested he would soon be displaying his flying wagon. A queue was already forming and Randolph mustered a friendly wave for Buck and Hodge at the gate and they mustered an unfriendly gesture in return. And then they were out on the open trail.

For the first five miles they maintained a brisk pace, both men eager to put Harvest Pass behind them, but when the trailing horse's wheezes started to drown out the sound of the creaking wagon, they slowed.

"Do you think we can get anywhere by sundown?" Fergal asked.

"Yeah, I reckon—"

A gunshot sounded, near and behind them.

Randolph peered around the side of the wagon to see three riders galloping toward them, and they all had their guns brandished. One man fired a speculative shot at them. It clattered yards wide, but Randolph still darted his head back, then shook the reins.

Their horses, which were used to having an angry mob pursue them out of town, surged ahead, but without the desperate speed that Randolph expected.

Then he remembered the trailing horse and winced.

Fergal saw his concern and leaned around the other side of the wagon, then darted back to report that the horse was lumbering and not making the achievement of speed very easy.

"We've got to cut it free," he said.

"We can't do that!" Randolph shouted. "We're a team!"

"A team with one very slow horse." Fergal considered Randolph's sneer. "Then put it this way—dead men don't own horses!"

"All right, but when we shake off these men, we will come back for it."

Fergal nodded and leaned around the side of the

wagon to cut the rope. The lead horses may have sensed this or the trailing horse may have been digging its heels in, but either way, the wagon surged on ahead, achieving a more familiar speed.

Despite their speed, when Randolph glanced back he saw that the following riders were still closing on them but the bay was stomping to a halt. Then, with apparent extreme stupidity, it wandered into the path of the oncoming riders.

The lead rider tried to avoid it but whichever way he tried to go the horse went that way, too, and he had to pull up completely to edge past it. And when the next rider tried to barge past, the horse backed into his path and the man only succeeded in uprooting himself from the saddle. The other rider surged off the trail and gave the horse a wide berth.

Randolph smiled as he rocked back into the seat.

"I can't work out whether that horse is the cleverest animal alive or the most stupid."

"Either way," Fergal said, grinning, "I reckon you're right and we need to go back for it later."

"Yeah, but when?"

Fergal gulped. "In about ten seconds is my guess."

"Ten sec—" Randolph winced and pulled back on the reins.

Ahead, a line of four riders was blocking the trail and they were close enough for Randolph to see the kerchiefs that were covering the lower half of their faces.

With a snap of the wrist, he turned the wagon in a short arc to head back down the trail toward Harvest Pass.

But off the trail the ground was rocky and he had to slow the wagon to a dawdling trot to avoid breaking the wheels. This gave one of the bandits enough time to hurry on and draw alongside.

Randolph passed the reins to Fergal then scrambled for his gun as he prepared to defend their wagon, but the man swung off his horse and leaped on to their lead horse.

This foolhardy maneuver shocked Randolph into not drawing his gun for a moment, but as he recovered and shouted out a warning the man drew a knife. Then, instead of trying to halt the horses, he reached back and, with a few deft slashes, cut through the rigging, freeing the horses from the wagon and rode them on.

"Now that was clever," Fergal murmured as the wagon rumbled to a halt. He watched their horses head off down the trail then dropped the slack reins. "We ain't going nowhere now."

"Then we've just got to make our stand here."

Randolph peered around the side of the wagon to see that the other riders in the trailing group were bearing down on them and ahead, the riders who had first chased them were closing fast.

Randolph raised his gun and took careful aim at the nearest rider, but from over the incline to their side, another three men appeared, swooping down on them and whooping a war cry.

"Or perhaps we do the other thing," Fergal murmured.

"Which is?"

"Run! We can get the wagon back another day."

Randolph glanced at the phalanx of bandits bearing down on them from three different directions and, with a nod, agreed that escaping with their lives was more important than protecting their property. He turned to head in the only direction from which the bandit gang wasn't attacking, and saw that Fergal was already hightailing it for cover.

Randolph jumped down from the wagon and surged after him, wheeling his arms as he fought for more speed. He expected gunfire from behind but when it didn't come he guessed that if the bandits' target had been the wagon, their flight was of little importance. He drew alongside Fergal as they hurried up a slight slope and, side by side, threw themselves over the top to lie flat.

Ahead lay miles of grasslands and no cover behind which they could hide, so they stayed where they were to watch what the bandits did next.

The bandits circled the wagon, some looking toward them, but just as one dismounted, gunfire blasted from nearby.

One bandit swung his gun round to aim up at them, and Randolph raised his gun to return fire, but Fergal slapped a hand on his arm, lowering his gun.

"Hey, bandits!" he shouted. "That wasn't us!"

Then Fergal ducked and threw his arms over his head as he cringed into a ball.

"Your bravery never ceases to amaze me," Randolph murmured as he looked around, searching for who had fired until he saw a line of riders galloping down the trail toward the wagon. He recognized many of them as coming from Harvest Pass, and leading the posse was Sheriff Johnson, with Jim and Lloyd close behind.

"That sure was quick," Fergal said, peering out from under an arm. "How did they learn that a bandit gang have just raided us?"

"I don't know, but that Jim and Lloyd are always mighty close whenever we face trouble."

Fergal shrugged. "Perhaps they're just protecting their investment."

"Perhaps."

The bandits spread out, but as the approaching posse outnumbered them by three to one a ripple of orders passed between them and they headed off into the hills, firing over their shoulders in a display of bravado.

Randolph waited until they were one hundred yards away, then rolled over the edge of the slope and hurried down to meet the oncoming posse, but it barely acknowledged him before swinging round to chase after the bandits.

"Whatever their reasoning," Randolph said, as

Fergal joined him, "we'd better hope they catch those bandits because we aren't going nowhere until we get our horses back."

"Or horse," Fergal said, looking back down the trail.

"We left that bay a long way back."

Fergal shook his head. "That horse is like a bad smell. We just ain't ever getting rid of it."

Randolph turned to follow Fergal's gaze and saw that he was right. Their other horse was mooching toward them at a leisurely pace with its tail swinging.

"Well, at least it'll get us back to Harvest Pass."

"Yeah," Fergal murmured. "And at least we ain't in a hurry."

Chapter Eight

"What are we going to do now?" Randolph asked, as he halted the wagon outside the same stable from which they'd departed, just two hours earlier.

As expected, it had been a slow journey back. Whatever spark of life had encouraged the horse to block the path of the bandits then hurry back to meet them had exhausted it for the day.

"I don't know," Fergal said, pointing down the road. "But I reckon things are still looking bad."

The posse was riding back into town, and judging by the men's sour expressions they had failed to catch the bandits. And, when the group dismounted outside the sheriff's office, Sheriff Johnson gave everyone a quick commiserating wave but drew Jim and Lloyd aside. They shared a lengthy conversation, punctuated with several long looks their way, then headed into the office.

"I wonder," Randolph said, "what the men who sold us the treasure of Saint Woody are talking about with the sheriff."

Fergal considered the sheriff's office, then Morgana's abandoned buckboard, then glanced over his shoulder to look at Ezekiel's show.

"I don't know. But I reckon it's time we worked out what's going on in Harvest Pass. Jim and Lloyd ain't the only ones who are acting suspiciously."

"Like who?"

"We have a man who sought us out to sell us a flying wagon just after Jim and Lloyd sold us a treasure casket. We have Ezekiel T Montgomery arriving in town along with a woman who steals from showmen. And now we have a bandit gang who were waiting outside town to raid us."

"And what do you care about suspicions?"

"When as many people as that are doing something suspicious, I reckon we've got a chance to make money." Fergal pointed down the road at the Lucky Star saloon. "So, I reckon you need to ask some more questions."

Randolph didn't need any further encouragement to jump down from the wagon.

In the next hour, he visited three saloons, the wanted posters outside the sheriff's office, another saloon, then the cemetery. He returned with some answers but far more questions.

Fergal was sitting on the back step of his wagon and peering into a crate. And the crate wasn't one Randolph recognized.

"You won't believe what I found in our wagon," Fergal said, looking up.

Randolph winced. "Everything is in there, isn't it?"

"Everything is, plus some things that weren't in there before."

Randolph glanced into the crate and withdrew a crown.

"What's this?"

Fergal waved a sheet of paper. "According to this list, that's King Arthur's crown and somewhere there's a sword called Excalibur."

"What's that?"

"No idea."

Randolph sat down beside Fergal. "But whatever it is, I guess Morgana was busy making her own authentic historical memorabilia."

"She wasn't." Fergal reached into the crate and removed a poster. "They were all previously owned by someone called Dewey Malone."

Randolph nodded. "That's the man who used to own our jeweled casket, except he's in a casket of his own right now."

"What happened?"

"Apparently an outlaw called Van Romalli happened." Randolph withdrew a wanted poster from his jacket and handed it to Fergal.

Fergal opened then considered the poster. On it was the fanciful depiction of a desperate looking man. He had a jagged scar across his cheek and squinting, close-together eyes that had clearly been drawn as a general depiction of a ruthless outlaw that nobody had actually seen. The offer was a two thousand dollar reward for the outlaw, Van Romalli.

"And you reckon he was with the bandits who were after us?"

"It's probable. Although everyone says he works alone." Randolph pointed at the bottom of the poster, which listed Romalli's raids. Prominently displayed was his enthusiasm for raiding showmen. "And he raided this store in White Springs, then headed west and killed Dewey Malone."

Fergal reached into the crate of King Arthur memorabilia and withdrew a broken table leg, then the edge of a rounded fragment of table. He fitted the two pieces together while nodding.

"And so the rest pieces together. After Morgana stole our wagon, she came across Dewey's abandoned wagon and took everything that Van Romalli had left."

"Except for the casket, which was too heavy."

"But after she'd left, Jim and Lloyd found the

wagon and they could move the casket. They sold it to us, not knowing what it really was." Fergal frowned. "But that doesn't explain why those bandits were after us."

Randolph reached into the wagon to pat the casket.

"Because we now own something that's valuable."

"It's not valuable enough to entice that many bandits. If they wanted money, why didn't they attack Ezekiel?"

"Because Ezekiel is well-protected, and because that's what they were supposed to do." Randolph leaned toward Fergal and lowered his voice. "When I asked around, I heard that two US marshals are in town, and they're hunting Van Romalli."

"And that means they're Jim and Lloyd." Fergal watched Randolph nod, then sighed. "And the casket is the bait for them to catch Van Romalli. And we own that bait."

Randolph rummaged through the crate, finding a chalice. He poked a finger through the hole in the bottom, shaking his head, then turned to Fergal.

"So, as we're trapped here until the lawmen catch those bandits," he said, keeping his voice neutral, "we might as well try to help Morgana."

"All right," Fergal said, taking the holed chalice from Randolph then swinging the crate back into the wagon.

Randolph flinched. "I didn't expect you to agree with that so easily."

"I do have a good side, Randolph. And besides, I have an idea." Fergal pointed at the wanted poster, his finger wavering beside the reward offer. "And I reckon Morgana might be more useful than I first thought."

"Where is she?" Fergal asked.

Sheriff Johnson pointed to the endmost cell in which a figure sat hunched up on a bunk, a shawl over her head, her knees clutched to her chest, her face turned to the wall.

In the gloom of the darkened interior, the other prisoners were wolfing through their dinners, but this prisoner hadn't touched her fatty stew which was congealing on a plate before the cell door. But at least the sheriff had given her the dignity of an empty cell between her and the first male prisoner.

"Morgana ain't talkative," Sheriff Johnson said. "But if you've got the time to waste, you can talk to her."

Fergal nodded and paced down the row of cells until he stood before the end cell. Randolph was at his side, and the two men stared through the bars, each sporting a smile.

The sheriff shrugged and wandered back to his desk.

"I see you're in trouble," Fergal said.

Morgana flinched but remained hunched and staring at the wall.

"Don't worry," Randolph said. "We're here to help."

Still she didn't respond.

"All right," Fergal said, "we'll cut this short. We know what you did."

Morgana turned her head from the wall and peered at them, then raised her eyebrows.

"Which is?" she asked, her voice low.

"You really did have the misfortune to encounter Van Romalli. He ran you off the trail, but when he realized you had nothing to steal he left you alone. We happened across you and you took advantage of our kindness, but then you found a man who hadn't been as lucky as you had been—Dewey Malone. You stole everything you could carry and headed here, planning to steal from Ezekiel T Montgomery. Am I right so far?"

She shrugged. "So, you figured out what I did and you're here to gloat. Now you've done that, go away."

"We won't. As Randolph said, we want to help you."

"I don't believe that." She flashed a thin smile. "Because I know what you did."

"Which is?"

"You planted that bag of money on me."

Fergal raised his eyebrows. "Prove it."

"I can't, but I do know you haven't had a pang of conscience. You're here because you think I have information on Van Romalli that'll help you collect his two thousand dollar reward."

Fergal blinked then threw his arms wide and provided a huge smile.

"I might be."

"And you can't leave town when Van Romalli is still at large."

"That might be relevant too."

She laughed and turned her head to the wall.

"Then you're as trapped as I am and I've got nothing to say to you."

Both men tried more coaxing, but they couldn't get her to turn and, if anything, she withdrew even further into her shawl.

Sheriff Johnson headed along the row of cells to join them.

"What will happen to her?" Fergal asked.

"She'll face Judge Perkins in a week, but unless Ezekiel T Montgomery comes over all clement like I reckon she's looking at a whole lot longer than a week in a cell."

Fergal and Randolph looked down the length of cells and shivered.

"Then we'd better have a word with this Ezekiel and see if we can encourage him to be more clement."

Johnson grunted. "Ezekiel won't listen. He wants her to suffer."

"It's still worth asking." Fergal spread his thin

arms wide revealing his bright green waistcoat. "I am a very persuasive man."

"I guess it won't hurt to try." Johnson narrowed his eyes. "But why are you trying to help her after everything she did to you?"

Fergal flinched. "You wound me with the suggestion that I have an ulterior motive. No woman should be in a cell."

Johnson nodded then gestured to the door.

"I guess you're right. I wish you luck."

"Wait!" a reedy voice said from the cell. All three men turned to see Morgana turn from the wall and, with the shawl still wrapped tightly around her head, peer back, her eyes bright in the shadows. "So, you really are going to try to help me whether I talk to you or not."

"I'll do anything I can to get you free," Fergal said.

Morgana nodded. "Did you say *anything*?"

Chapter Nine

Morgana stayed quiet until Sheriff Johnson left them. Then she fixed Fergal with a steady glare through the bars.

"Here's the deal," she said, talking with a quick and level tone that didn't offer room for negotiation. "Nobody knows what Van Romalli looks like except for me. And I also learnt something when he raided me, something that would help an ambitious man to find him."

Fergal uttered a low laugh. "We'd prefer not to find Van Romalli. We want to know how to avoid him."

"But a bounty hunter or someone with more imagination than Sheriff Johnson might be interested."

"He might. So, make your offer and I'll consider it."

"It's simple—get me out of this cell and I'll tell you what Van Romalli looks like and where he's currently hiding out."

Fergal smiled. "Then it's a deal."

He and Morgana looked at each other and, in their gazes, Randolph reckoned he saw something, perhaps mutual respect, but Fergal was the first to turn away. Randolph smiled at her, receiving a sweet smile in return, then hurried after Fergal.

On the boardwalk, he joined Fergal in leaning on the hitching rail.

"How do you reckon you can get Ezekiel to drop the charges against her?"

"Don't know yet." Fergal pushed himself up from the rail and pointed at the people who were heading out of town. "But I know one thing for sure, I ain't telling him I was the one who stole from him. Come on. We're paying our first visit to the greatest show on all the Earth."

Randolph and Fergal exchanged a sneer and headed down the road.

As this was the third day of Ezekiel's show, fewer people than before were heading out of town to see it and, as the first show was two hours away, they entered without Buck and Hodge noticing them.

Around the central corral and tent was a circle of attractions. Milton Moon's wagons were behind the main tent, although as yet there was still no sign of his attraction.

As they wandered around, each man offered supportive comments to the other, stating that the attractions Ezekiel was offering weren't as good as the attractions they had in their authentic historical memorabilia exhibition.

After a complete tour, and still feeling unimpressed, they stopped before the attraction that had enticed the most people.

Three large nails were set out on the ground, each twenty feet farther away than the previous nail. After paying a dime, the punter had to hurl three horseshoes and snag them on the nails to win ten dollars.

This attraction had lured five men, who stepped up to try their luck, paid their dimes, and received three horseshoes. But after they'd all tried, only two had snagged the first two nails and the third remained elusive.

But when they'd all tried a second time, one of the men declared that he now had that final nail in his sights and bought another go.

"Fool," Fergal murmured.

"I reckon he's got a chance," Randolph said, appraising the man's confident stance.

"We've got more chance of getting into the treasure of Saint Woody than he has of snagging that third nail."

The first horseshoe sailed through the air and clinked to a halt around the first nail.

"You telling me that it's impossible to get three horseshoes around those nails?"

"Sure is."

The second horseshoe snagged on the second nail and the man adjusted his position a foot to the left and began a steady up and down motion of the arm as he prepared to throw.

"That third nail is a good sixty feet away, but I don't reckon it's impossible."

"Watch."

The man hurled the third horseshoe. It sailed up in the air, then came down, heading straight for the nail. The watching men gasped with a collective sigh and, when the horseshoe came down, it snagged around the nail, spinning round and round. A huge whoop of delight went up then died in mid-whoop as the nail fell over, tumbling the horseshoe away.

As a potential punchup between the unsuccessful thrower and the attraction's owner started then died out when Buck and Hodge strolled over to the stall, Fergal led Randolph away.

"All right," Randolph said, "but all these attractions can't be crooked." Randolph pointed at the display beyond the horseshoe game. "That one can't be a trick, surely."

Fergal glanced at the sign for the attraction, then winced.

"Guess the number of legs on a cow," he read,

"only one dollar a go. Win twenty-five dollars for a correct guess."

As they shook their heads, they watched a group of men who stood before the offer, reading and re-reading it as Fergal and Randolph had, and muttering their disbelief to each other. Then one of the men paid his dollar. He was biting his bottom lip to avoid grinning as he wrote his guess on a slip of paper. Then he slipped under the awning to see whether he was right.

A minute later, he emerged shaking his head with his shoulders hunched.

"Wasn't even close," he murmured when he re-joined his group.

"I've got only one thought about a place like this," Randolph said.

"Yeah, it's guaranteed to make a fortune."

They watched the bad guesser receive commiserations from his colleagues, but then one of the group had a good idea. With a nonchalant air, he traded whispers with the unsuccessful guesser. They exchanged a few nods, grins and even a greedy rub of the hands. Then the second man headed to the stall, paid his money, and made his informed *guess*.

Then he went in.

Randolph and Fergal watched, wondering how they'd avoid paying him now that he knew the answer, but he emerged a few moments later shaking his head.

"Still not even close," he said.

Randolph sighed. "For all the glamour of this place, it still comes down to these sorts of attractions."

"Ezekiel has to earn his money somehow to pay for the real attractions."

"Perhaps, but do you reckon you can persuade a man who runs a place like this to release Morgana?"

Fergal rolled his shoulders. "He'll agree to anything I say, and I'll stake my reputation on that. Stay here and try not to lose any money. I have some serious negotiating to do."

As Fergal headed into the main tent, Randolph went on another circuit of the stalls. But then he noticed Buck and Hodge, who were supervising an attraction in which you had to knock a large metal cube off a wide podium with three wet rags. This unlikely feat had gained plenty of interest on account of the thousand dollar prize for whoever managed it. He circled away and found himself standing before what had to be the most honest attraction in the whole show.

All he had to do was shoot the pips out of four aces to win ten dollars. Randolph fished in his pocket for a nickel.

"This can't be crooked," he whispered to himself, "surely."

Inside the tent, Fergal faced the white-clad Ezekiel T Montgomery for the first time. The showman sat at a desk in the corner of his tent. A huge pile of papers coated the desk, many being posters for various attractions. Behind an awning at his side, industrious noises and the occasional curse emerged, Fergal recognizing the voice as being Moon's.

"I'm a busy man," Ezekiel said, not looking up from his consideration of a poster. "Make this quick."

"I intend to," Fergal said. "We have a problem."

"Do *we*?"

"A young lady is in a jail cell facing a lengthy sentence and neither of us want her to suffer that."

"That is not true, and I don't see why that's your problem." Ezekiel looked up for the first time. "Or even mine."

"It is a long story and I won't bore you with it, but I will ask you to drop the charges against her."

"I am not doing that." Ezekiel looked down with studied finality.

"And for a man who is trying to appear as a jovial showman to the townsfolk of Harvest Pass, that isn't wise. If you were magnanimous and—"

Ezekiel raised a hand. "I hear what you're saying and I'm just not interested."

"Then let us talk business." Fergal held his hands wide.

"You want to strike a deal with me?" Ezekiel looked up and appraised Fergal with his bright eyes gleaming. He watched Fergal nod, then laughed. "All right. I will let her go for one thousand dollars."

Fergal had firmed his jaw and kept his face impassive at this wild opening offer.

"Morgana didn't steal that much money from you."

"How do you know how much she stole?"

Fergal gulped. "Sheriff Johnson is a talkative man."

Ezekiel narrowed his eyes a moment, then glanced down at his poster again.

"He is and he has told me much about you. And I'll tell you why you're really here. Van Romalli is in the hills, looking to raid little men like you. Morgana had a close encounter with him and she has information on his location. She's promised to tell you that information if you convince me to let her go."

Fergal let a smile appear for the first time since entering the tent.

"You are a perceptive man."

"And I am a successful man and that's something you'll never be."

"I have my moments and today, I have something to bargain with." Fergal lowered his voice. "I know about some other people who are after Van Romalli."

"Is that other than the U.S. Marshals Jim Broughton and Lloyd Henderson?"

Fergal couldn't help but let the corner of his mouth twitch.

"No, but as I know them, I can use them to stop Van Romalli raiding you."

"Romalli will never raid me. I am too well-protected."

"Buck and Hodge aren't much of a defense against the likes of Van Romalli."

"They take care of the minor nobodies such as yourself and Randolph. For the more serious foes, I have more serious protection. You have not seen my show, but I have real heroes: Men who can shoot a fly off a man's nose at one hundred paces."

"Randolph can do that."

"Without using a gun?"

Fergal blinked. "How?"

Ezekiel favored Fergal with his dazzling smile.

"Come and see the show and you'll find out, but that's just the start. I have the best riders, the strongest men and the finest shots you'll find anywhere and the likes of Van Romalli wouldn't take me on unless he wanted to smell a whole heap of lead."

"There must be something you want that I can provide."

"A little man like you has nothing to offer a great man like me." Ezekiel shrugged, then lowered his voice and, hidden behind his sneering tone, Fergal detected genuine intrigue. "Although I wonder why you own the treasure of Saint Woody, an attraction that Dewey Malone had promised to sell to me."

Fergal clenched his jaw to avoid reacting to this revelation.

"It is a fascinating story as to how I obtained this

fabulous attraction, but if you still want it we could reach an agreement."

"I might once have been interested but now I have something that's far more exciting." He leaned over the desk and presented Fergal with a ticket. "Come along tomorrow and see how the real showmen amaze the public."

Fergal glanced at the ticket, but then sneered and folded his arms.

"I've seen your attractions outside. And guessing the number of legs on a cow doesn't amaze me."

"Then read this." Ezekiel held out a rolled up poster.

This time, Fergal took the poster and flicked it open to see a picture of a wagon led by four white horses. On the seat, its driver stood in an heroic pose with one leg thrust forward and his muscular arm cracking a whip above the horses. But none of this was as surprising as the fact that the wagon was at least a hundred feet off the ground and the two wings on its side were flapping it off into a deep red sunset.

"You really have bought Milton Moon's flying wagon!" Fergal laughed. "And there was me thinking that you were an astute showman."

"I am, and this is the greatest attraction there has ever been for the greatest show there has ever been."

"But this wagon has wings and I've heard that Milton's flying wagon does not."

"When I am promoting the show, the wagon will

have wings." Ezekiel leaned to the side and lifted a corner of the awning. "Won't it, Milton?"

Milton Moon emerged from behind the awning, his arms black with soot and his large glasses steamed up. He removed them and gave them a furious polish.

"I keep telling you, the wings will spoil my carefully constructed—"

"Yeah, yeah, but if the customers expect wings, they'll get wings."

"They only expect wings because you've put them on the poster." Milton considered the poster, then put his glasses back on and cocked his head to one side. "Although the wagon driver is a good likeness . . . Anyhow, nobody has any expectation of what a flying wagon will look like because before today nobody in Harvest Pass will have seen one."

"Wings, give me wings." Ezekiel stood and held his arms aloft. "I can see it now. It'll soar. It'll swoop."

Ezekiel circled on the spot with his arms outstretched, doing, in Fergal's opinion, a passable impression of an eagle.

"My flying wagon won't soar and it won't swoop," Milton muttered, his sullen tone suggesting this wasn't the first time they'd had this discussion. "It'll be more like the stately progress of a—"

"Who is promoting your invention?"

"You are." Milton turned to leave. "And I guess

it'll soar and it'll swoop, and people will pay a lot of money to see it."

"On that we can both agree." Ezekiel turned to Fergal and smiled. "So, you see? You have nothing to offer a man who is promoting a flying wagon."

Fergal considered his fingernails, then buffed them on his jacket.

"In my years as a successful showman, I've seen many attractions that are far better than that."

Ezekiel snorted. "What's better than a flying wagon?"

"Lots of things. Where I come from, everyone has a flying wagon and there ain't nothing special about seeing one of those."

Ezekiel narrowed his eyes, but when Fergal just returned his gaze with his level stare, he shook his head.

"They do not."

Fergal folded his arms and held his chin high.

"And they sure do. Flying is easy."

"Is it?"

"It sure is."

Ezekiel slapped both hands on his desk and leaned forward. The dazzling smile appeared and the eyes gleamed.

"Then maybe I do have a proposition for you that'll get Morgana out of jail."

Thirty minutes after Fergal had headed into the tent, Randolph was fighting a losing battle to avoid trying the shooting attraction, but then he saw Fergal emerging from the tent with his head held low.

Randolph reckoned it was now or never and paced up to the stall, but Fergal hurried to his side and slammed a hand on his arm.

"Don't be fooled by that," he said.

"But I've only got to shoot the pips out of those cards. And they will let me use my own gun. What kind of trick can they pull on that?"

"And that's the skill in the trick. But we ain't wasting money to find out." Fergal turned to the gates and paced off. "Come on. We have work to do."

Randolph hurried after Fergal. "Have you got a deal out of Ezekiel?"

"I sure have. I've taken a wager with him. And he's letting Morgana go straight away."

Randolph blew out his cheeks. "Well negotiated."

"And if I win the wager, he'll give me all the money he'll earn from tomorrow's show of Milton Moon's flying wagon. It could be around one thousand dollars."

"Even better negotiated."

"But if I lose, I lose everything: The treasure of Saint Woody, the historical memorabilia, the tonic, the wagon, everything."

Randolph gulped. "High stakes indeed. What's the wager?"

Fergal stopped beside the gates and turned to Randolph, but he looked over his shoulder.

"It'll take some effort but it's a wager we can win."

"But what is it?"

"It needs us to be more ingenious than we have ever been before."

"All right but what do we have to do?"

Fergal threw his hands aloft. "We must astound and amaze with our daring."

"Yes," Randolph grunted. He clamped a hand on each of Fergal's shoulders and shook him, lowering his arms. "But doing *what*?"

Fergal took a deep breath and looked at Randolph.

"We have twenty-four hours to learn how to fly or we lose everything."

Chapter Ten

"Learn how to fly?" Randolph shouted, hurling his arms wide and looming over Fergal as his anger got the better of him.

"Yeah," Fergal said, stepping back, "Milton's assembled his flying wagon. It's tomorrow's big attraction. But I got irritated with the smug way Ezekiel rebuffed everything I offered him so I challenged Milton to a race."

"In the air?" Randolph blustered, exasperated at Fergal's reckless wager.

"You got it. And it's only over a quarter-mile across that lake. And from what Milton was saying, his flying wagon doesn't go very fast."

Randolph slapped a hand over his eyes while he forced himself to calm down. When he no longer felt like giving Fergal his first flying lesson with a well-placed kick, he tried one last time to make him see sense.

"I've got news for you, Fergal. That ain't the problem. No matter how fast he goes, we won't be getting off the ground." He ground his teeth, forcing down another flash of anger. "So what are the exact rules of this wager?"

"The first person to touch dry earth on the other side of the lake without any part of his flying wagon touching the water is the winner." Fergal narrowed his eyes as he considered Randolph's sudden smile. "Going around the sides won't count. We have to be inventive here."

"No matter how inventive we might be, does it not bother you that as far as I know no man has ever got off the ground before, and we have just one day to learn how to do it?"

"No." Fergal smiled. "I always win."

"And how can you win at flying?"

"I don't know." Fergal rubbed his chin, then blew out his cheeks. "But Milton can do it, so just how hard can it be?"

"When will you free Morgana?" Fergal asked Sheriff Johnson when they arrived back in town.

"Already done that," Johnson said, pointing at the empty cell in the corner. "And now she's left town."

"Left . . ." Fergal flinched in surprise then slammed

his hands on his hips. "That sure was ungrateful after everything I've just done."

"She said you didn't mind."

"Well, she can't have got far." Fergal turned to the door, but Johnson coughed, and he turned back.

"She probably has. We found one of the horses those bandits stole from you. She left on it." Johnson smiled. "She said you didn't mind."

Fergal winced. "And did you not think that someone who steals as often as she does might have been lying?"

"Nope. You and her had been getting on just fine, and you did get Ezekiel to drop the charges."

"Don't remind me." Fergal headed to the door. "I'm regretting it already."

Johnson watched him leave, then turned to Randolph.

"She left you a message though." Johnson extracted a letter from his pocket then passed it to Randolph.

As Randolph followed Fergal out, he read the legend on the back of the envelope, then jumped up on to their wagon to join Fergal.

"Morgana says she doesn't know where Van Romalli will be when you read this," he said, then passed the envelope to Fergal. "But she does know where he's been for the last few days."

Fergal nodded. "Hopefully, that'll be enough."

He sliced open the envelope and extracted the single

piece of paper from within. He read the short note, then re-read it. Then he sneered, crumpled it into a ball, and threw it over his shoulder.

Randolph watched Fergal snort his breath through his nostrils, then offered him a smile.

"Did she say anything that'll help catch Van Romalli?"

"Perhaps, but not any time soon." Fergal turned to Randolph and frowned. "The message was: When Van Romalli has gone only Angus is left."

The horse whinnied then rolled the wagon forward a pace, forcing Randolph to grab the reins and yank them back.

"What does that mean?"

"I've got no idea and I ain't in the mood for riddles."

"But I guess it'd help to know who this Angus is."

Again the horse bristled and Fergal blew out his cheeks as he tipped back his hat.

"It would, but I reckon the horse has heard that name before."

Both men stared down at the bay, but for once the horse stayed looking forward.

"Pity it can't speak, then."

"And you reckon this will work, do you?" Randolph asked as he stared down the slope at the lake below.

"Of course it will," Fergal said. He slapped the

buckboard seat on either side of him, then pointed down the hill, but when Randolph didn't move them off, he provided a more realistic shrug. "But I guess it can go two ways."

Randolph raised the reins. "The only way this flying wagon is going is down."

Randolph maneuvered the buckboard around so that it pointed straight down the slope toward the lake. They faced a slope of about two hundred yards before they reached the water, but the last fifty yards had a considerable incline.

"We'll go down first of all, but then we'll go up."

Randolph sighed. It had been a long day that had been filled with inventive thought interspersed with painful bumps.

As Morgana hadn't told them how they could avoid Van Romalli, they had no choice but to stay in town and try to win Fergal's reckless wager. So, they had sat beside the lake and watched birds fly past. Then they'd spent several hours trying to build wings that were no more successful in getting them off the ground than they had been when they'd ran in circles jumping up and down and flapping their arms.

Then they'd lain on their backs and watched the birds glide and this had led to them devoting several hours to nailing planks together, followed by several more hours nursing bruises.

But Fergal had noticed how Randolph's jacket had billowed out behind him just before he'd hit the ground and this had led to a grandiose plan that took up the rest of the day. And now, with sundown approaching, they sat on their specially rigged out buckboard ready for their maiden flight.

The middle planks of the buckboard's side boards stuck out at right angles—for gliding once they were airborne. The cloth from the buckboard splayed out behind them—for a softer landing. And the speed to get airborne would come from the slope to the lake.

Randolph shook the reins. "Come on, Pegasus."

"Pegasus?"

"The horse needs a name and it's mythological—a winged horse."

"The horse won't be flying, we will be."

"That don't matter. I reckon neither of us will be."

"Stop being so pessimistic. The key to flying is for the horse to get us enough speed before we release it."

Both men considered the bow-legged horse. It was munching grass, pausing only to wheeze.

"Then perhaps we need to find another horse."

Fergal nodded but before he could alight, Pegasus lifted his head and set off at a reasonable pace.

They rocked back and forth as they trundled down the hill, the slope letting Pegasus achieve an unheard of speed, but Randolph yanked the reins to the side, veering Pegasus off at an angle to the lake.

"Ready with stage one?" he asked.

"Ready," Fergal said.

Randolph watched the start of the steepest part of the slope approach and, ten yards away from it, grunted the order.

Fergal pulled back on the rope they'd looped around the rigging and the whole rigging fell away, letting Pegasus hurry off on his own. But they continued rolling without him and, as they rumbled over the edge of the steep part of the slope, they veered off to take the most direct course to the lake.

Free now, they built up speed, hurtling on toward the water's edge. Randolph glanced back to see the wind was whipping the cloth and it was standing upright as they'd expected, and when Randolph turned back he saw that the water was just forty yards away. And they were heading for the exact spot they'd aimed for—a flat length of rock that was flush to the slope, but which provided a ten-foot drop to the water.

"When you reckon we'll start flying?" he shouted.

"It'll be about fifty yards, I reckon," Fergal shouted back.

"We're closer to the lake than that already."

"Then," Fergal screeched, slamming his hands over his head, "we might have ourselves a problem."

Ten minutes later, both men sat on the edge of the rock, dangling their legs over the water.

The back of the buckboard protruded from the lake, about fifteen feet in. Pegasus had mooched down the slope to peer over their shoulders and periodically nudged Randolph, encouraging him to retrieve the buckboard, but as yet, Randolph was more interested in drying his clothes.

"You know," Fergal mused, "I reckon we nearly flew there."

"Was that *before* we nearly drowned?"

"I reckon it was."

"And was that *after* you screamed?"

"That was a whoop of bravado."

"Was that what it was? Then perhaps we should drag the buckboard out and have another go. Perhaps if we could get even more speed, we might fly for another five feet."

Fergal jumped to his feet and stared across the water at the hill on the other side, a quarter-mile on.

"No," he said, rubbing his hands, "I reckon we got just far enough to win this race."

Contented whistling was emerging from Ezekiel's tent as Fergal glanced at Randolph, receiving a shrug.

"Surely," Fergal whispered, "they should all be in bed by now. It must be after midnight."

Randolph looked at the low, gibbous moon.

"Perhaps the flying wagon isn't as finalized as Milton claimed it was."

Fergal grinned and shook his medical bag. Inside, the collection of hammers and knives rattled.

"And after we've finished with it, it never will be

again." Fergal winked. "And our flying wagon will get the farthest across the lake."

"Even if that is only fifteen feet."

Fergal laughed then gestured for Randolph to join him in slipping under the tent. They lay on their bellies with their heads poking through.

Inside, Milton had assembled his flying wagon, or at least they assumed that's what he'd done. At first sight, the wagon appeared to be nothing more than a heap of metal and silk. Milton was pattering over an expanse of bright green and red silk in his bare feet and examining every inch with his head held low.

In the center of the silk there was a metal frame set into a wicker basket. Along the length of the frame, there was a pipe, bent at five-foot intervals, which Randolph decided was a crank that needed two men to turn it. And at the end of the crank, there was a circular arrangement of blades that Randolph assumed would turn when the crank turned.

"He's put more thought into his flying wagon than we did," he said.

Fergal chuckled. "This isn't a battle for who puts the most thought into their design. It's a race."

"Still, that looks like something that could get off the ground."

"*Could* is the right word." Fergal patted the medical bag at his side. "But after a few modifications, I don't reckon it's going anywhere."

Randolph nodded, but then heard footfalls behind

him, and they were closing. He glanced at Fergal, but Fergal was already swinging his legs out from under the tent bottom and Randolph joined him in rolling free.

They lay a moment, in open view of anyone looking their way, but Milton was intent on checking his flying wagon. So, they rolled to their feet and scurried around the sides of the tent to reach the desk before which Fergal had made his foolhardy wager.

They hunkered down, hiding behind the desk, but then the tent billowed out at the spot where they'd been hiding and Buck and Hodge rolled through. As they extricated themselves, Fergal and Randolph rolled to the side and lay on their bellies.

"Did you see them?" Buck asked.

Milton grunted without looking round. "See who?"

"Those varmints, Fergal and Randolph. They were peeking in here."

"I have nothing to hide. It has taken me twenty years to perfect this design. They will not be able to replicate it in a day."

"Double-crossing showmen like them won't look to build a better flying wagon. They're planning to wreck your wagon."

Milton turned to face Buck. "Why would they do that?"

"Because then the wager will be off."

Randolph glanced around the side of the desk to

see Buck standing with his hands on his hips, considering Milton. Then Buck directed Hodge to search around the perimeter of the tent, while he paced in the opposite direction, heading straight toward them.

Lying on his belly, Randolph nudged Fergal.

"Doesn't look like we'll be sabotaging the flying wagon tonight."

"It don't, and we need to run."

"You're right." Randolph pointed to the exit. "On the count of three, run for it."

Fergal nodded. "Three."

Then Fergal was on his feet and hurtling for the exit, his long legs pounding as he displayed his second greatest talent—running from trouble.

Randolph was on his feet in a moment and pounding after him. He glanced at Buck, who did a double-take then hurried after him, gesturing frantically to Hodge to try to cut them off. But Hodge was twenty yards away and Buck was the only one who stood a chance.

Fergal pushed through the tent door but as Randolph followed him out, his foot slipped and he lost valuable seconds righting himself. This gave Buck enough time to put on a burst of speed and pile into him. He hit Randolph in the midriff and carried him back three paces before both men crashed to the ground.

All the air blasted from Randolph's lungs as he slammed on his back, but he used Buck's momentum and kept the roll going, throwing Buck over his side.

Buck hit the ground but he had a grip of Randolph's chest and the two men rolled then flopped to a halt.

Randolph was the first to stagger to his feet and he stumbled a pace, but Buck grabbed a trailing foot and hung on. Randolph still dragged him across the ground, but he could hear cloth rustling as Hodge pushed the tent flap aside. In a desperate act, he dropped to his knees, pivoted, and sat.

He kicked out, knocking Buck's hands away, then rolled backward, but he saw Hodge take a long running dive at him, aiming to bundle him on to his back. Randolph just had time to hurl himself to the side, Hodge landing on the ground on his belly, and then he was off, pounding into the night.

He heard Buck calling for Hodge to shoot him, but Randolph thrust his head down and hurried on. But as his eyes adjusted to the darkness, he failed to see Fergal.

He looked to the gates but still didn't see him, then saw two men standing by a stall to his side. One man was thin and held his hands high. Randolph had just registered that this was Fergal when he saw that the other man had a gun drawn and aimed at Fergal's back.

And this man wore a star on his chest—Sheriff Johnson.

Randolph skidded to a halt and, when the sheriff gestured for him to join Fergal, he raised his hands.

"You," Johnson said, "are under arrest."

"What for?" Fergal said, venturing a smile.

"I don't exactly know." Johnson raised his eyebrows as he glanced over Randolph's shoulder at Buck and Hodge. "But once I've talked with these men, I reckon I can find a few dozen things you've done wrong in the last few hours."

Chapter Eleven

As the sun filtered through the window bars on what should have been race day, Randolph looked into the opposite cell.

Fergal returned his stare along with an ironic smile that acknowledged that they wouldn't be getting out of these cells any time soon.

"What you reckon he'll charge us with?" Randolph asked.

Fergal shrugged then pointed, drawing his attention to the fact that Marshal Jim Broughton had just come into the sheriff's office. He spoke quietly with the sheriff, their frequent glances at Randolph and Fergal confirming the subject of their discussion. At first the sheriff set his jaw firm and shook his head but as Jim continued to speak, a slow smile spread.

"Not sure what crime we committed," Fergal said when Jim left the office and the sheriff made his way over to them. "Stopping a flying wagon from flying ain't that common."

"*Trying* to stop. We never got anywhere near that wagon."

Fergal leaned back on his bunk with his hands locked behind his head.

"Never mind, look on the bright side. If we're in here, at least we won't have to go through with that wager."

"There is that, although I . . ." Randolph trailed off when Sheriff Johnson stopped before Fergal's cell and waved a key at them.

Without acknowledging either man, he unlocked Fergal's door and held on to it as he peered inside.

"I've got me a choice," he muttered, his tone low and irritated. "Either I keep you in here until you rot, or I run you out of town."

"If we have a choice," Fergal said, smiling, "we'll stay here."

"I thought you might say that. So, I reckon you're leaving."

Fergal gulped. "But are you aware that Van Romalli's out there, waiting to pray on innocent showmen like us?"

"I am. And that's why I'm letting you go." Johnson strode into the cell, grabbed Fergal's arm, and yanked him to his feet. "But don't worry, if Romalli finds you after you've lost everything in the race, I'll bury whatever he leaves behind."

With Fergal grumbling at every pace, Johnson dragged him to the door and outside.

Randolph pressed his face to the bars and watched Johnson release Fergal, then boot him off the boardwalk. Fergal rolled to his feet and hurried back to face the sheriff, but with a steady shake of the head Johnson was the first to turn away and head back into his office.

After Fergal's treatment, Randolph slipped through the opened cell door quietly. Even so, a kick from Johnson hurried him on. Running a few paces ahead of Johnson's firm boot, he dashed outside to join an irritated Fergal on the boardwalk.

"So," he said, "I guess we are leaving town."

Fergal glanced around until he saw Jim and Lloyd standing on the other side of the road watching them. He gave Jim a short bow in acknowledgment of his efforts in getting them free, even if it had an obvious ulterior motive, then headed down the boardwalk to their wagon.

"I guess we are." A smile appeared. "But as you said, if Johnson is running us out of town, we don't have to lose that race."

Randolph shook his head. "The lake isn't in town."

Fergal stopped. "Are you sure?"

Randolph looked down the road toward the edge

of town, then at the hills where the race would take place this afternoon.

"I reckon so."

Fergal nodded to himself as he rubbed his chin.

"In that case," he murmured, "I guess you'd better go to the lake and start building another flying wagon."

"Aren't you helping?"

"No." Fergal headed for the wagon. "I'm heading out of town for a while."

"You're forgetting something, Fergal. Van Romalli is still out there, and those marshals are hoping he'll raid you when you leave town."

"I haven't forgotten." Fergal stopped before his wagon, then turned to Randolph, smiling. "I'm counting on it."

Fergal pulled the wagon to a halt and peered around. He was five miles out of Harvest Pass and at the place where the bandits had raided him. He hadn't caught sight of Jim and Lloyd but he assumed they were close by.

Aside from the fact that Fergal had placed the treasure of Saint Woody on the seat beside him, nothing had changed since the last time he'd left town.

After waiting for ten minutes, from ahead, a line of five riders crested the hill and, as they closed, Fergal saw that they were brandishing guns and had kerchiefs wrapped over the lower parts of their faces.

"Reach," the lead rider said, drawing his horse to a halt, twenty yards before Pegasus.

Fergal raised his hands to shoulder level.

"Are you Van Romalli?" he asked.

"You don't ask the questions," the bandit grunted. "And you've got ten seconds to get off that wagon or I'll fill you full of holes."

"I'll get off but I've got nothing for you to steal."

The eyes above the kerchief narrowed. Then the bandit pointed with his gun at the wagon.

"You've got to have something worth stealing in there."

"I haven't." Fergal slapped the casket lid. "This is worthless."

The bandit shrugged. "Then you'll have something else that's valuable."

Fergal flinched. "You mean you ain't after the treasure of Saint Woody?"

"There's a saint called Woody?"

"There is." Fergal stood. "But answer my question—are you after this box?"

The bandit gestured with his gun to the ground.

"Get down now or die!"

Fergal moved to jump down from his wagon but stopped and raised a finger.

"I am right. You aren't after this, but as Van Romalli is supposed to be after this box that means you ain't anything to do with Van Romalli."

"Last warning." The bandit snorted a laugh. "I can search you just as quickly dead as alive."

"You can, but you haven't got much time." Fergal pointed over his shoulder and back along the trail toward Harvest Pass. "Marshal Jim Broughton and Deputy Lloyd Henderson are behind me, ready to pounce when you've raided me."

As one, the bandits drew their horses back a pace, each man darting his gaze around.

"You led us into a trap." The lead man sighted Fergal down the barrel of his gun.

"Not by design," Fergal said, his tone unconcerned despite the gun. "You've got enough time to get away before the lawmen arrive. They're some way behind me I reckon."

The bandit's gun arm wavered then inch by inch he lowered it.

"Telling me that the lawmen won't be here in time to rescue you was either mighty stupid or mighty odd."

"It was just sensible when I want a deal. Because, you see, this casket is the bait to catch Van Romalli, except I don't like owning bait, and it don't even interest you."

"Bait or no bait, hand over your wagon."

"I can hand it over, but like I said, I've got no money to give you." As the bandit grunted an oath, Fergal raised a hand. "But as you ain't Van Romalli I do have something that's even better than money."

"Ain't nothing better than money."

"There is." Fergal provided his largest and most friendly smile. "Information."

The bandit glanced at the other men, receiving the response of several raised eyebrows. He glanced at his gun then, with a twirl of his arm, holstered it.

"I'm listening," he said.

Randolph sat beside the lake. An hour earlier, he'd dragged the buckboard out of the lake and now it had dried, but it stood at an angle, the rickety wheels even more rickety after its plunge into the water.

And an idea as to how to build a flying wagon still felt as far away as it ever had.

On the opposite side of the lake, preparations to get Milton Moon's flying wagon into the air were well under way. An army of helpers was spreading out the silk and a steady stream of other townsfolk was emerging from town to see the wonder take shape.

Randolph tore his gaze away from the industrious activity and looked ahead, then smiled on seeing that Fergal was riding toward him.

He jumped to his feet and beckoned Fergal to hurry, but Pegasus still trundled him on at the same dawdling pace.

"Where you been?" he shouted.

"Trying to find a way for us to leave town," Fergal said as he pulled the wagon to a halt.

Randolph sighed. "And?"

"I think I might have done it," Fergal said, joining Randolph. "And if I have, all our problems are over."

Randolph raised his eyebrows, and when Fergal just shrugged, he grabbed his shoulders and turned him round to face all the activity happening on the other side of the lake.

"You're forgetting our main problem. We only have three hours left to learn how to fly."

"Three hours is a long time. I'm sure we'll think of something."

"But if we can't win by cheating, or by sabotage, or by running away, what can we do?"

Fergal looked at Pegasus. "I suppose we could try to get more speed out of the horse."

Pegasus looked up from his grass munching, muttered a snorting wheeze, then returned to his feeding.

"We can't do that. It prefers to just bumble along behind . . ."

Fergal considered the wide grin that was spreading across Randolph's face.

"Have you just had an idea?"

"Sure have."

Fergal looked at the horse, then at the lake, then at the buckboard. He shook his head.

"Sorry. I don't know what you're thinking, Randolph."

Randolph just winked.

Chapter Twelve

With the race just two hours away, the crowd had gathered to see what Ezekiel T Montgomery had optimistically billed as the greatest race of all time, and which Buck and Hodge had promised would be the best belly laugh of the year.

Milton had already laid out the huge expanse of silk to his satisfaction. Then he'd expanded it using a special gas, which he claimed was his own invention, but which was highly flammable. One look at the huge envelope had encouraged everyone to back away and, within an hour, it had taken shape and billowed into the air. And despite the lack of the wings that Ezekiel had promised, many said that the sight of his flying wagon rising into the air was worth the ten-dollar-a-head entrance fee alone.

After this, the bets ran wild on the result of the race. Standing in the shadow of the airborne wagon, most people wanted to bet on Milton getting across the lake.

Nobody took the bet that Fergal would win the race, although increasingly, everyone glanced around, looking for Fergal's arrival.

As the race approached, Ezekiel started fidgeting inside his white suit, as the likelihood that Fergal had run away became greater. He was just starting to flash glares at Buck and Hodge when Fergal's wagon came into view, trundling around the edge of the lake. Trailing along was the rickety buckboard.

The buckboard was painted white and when it was closer, everyone could see the recently painted depiction of an eagle on the side.

"So," Ezekiel said as Fergal pulled up his wagon, "you came. I thought you'd probably run away."

"I'd never do that," Fergal said. "I'm looking forward to winning our one thousand dollar bet."

"I thought you did this to free Morgana?"

"I am, but the prize money and the chance to wipe that blinding smile off your face will help too."

"You've got a chance to do that—a snowball in a fire's chance." Ezekiel threw back his head and guffawed.

Fergal was sneering when Ezekiel looked at him again. Then he stood aside as Randolph unhitched then dragged the buckboard around the side of the wagon. Their arrival encouraged Milton to hurry away from his preparations to join them.

Fergal placed himself on the edge of the huge shadow.

"And is that your flying wagon, Milton?" he asked, pointing upwards.

Milton snorted. "None other."

"I thought it'd be bigger."

Milton's eyes flared behind his glasses. "It is the largest balloon ever built and has the most sophisticated steering mechanism yet devised. Nobody has built one to carry three men before and the speed we will achieve will astound."

Fergal shrugged. "Either way, something that size will never beat my sleeker flying wagon."

Milton glanced around. "And where is your sleeker flying wagon?"

Fergal pointed at the buckboard. "Here it is, and as you can see, it's small and sleek."

Milton uttered a sharp snort as Ezekiel uttered a louder retort.

"That's no flying wagon."

"Not yet it isn't. We've still got to finish building it." Fergal slapped the side of the buckboard. "But we've got the most important job done—we've painted it. And when the paint's dry, we'll finish off our innovative new design."

"You've painted it," Ezekiel intoned, glancing at

Milton, whose mouth was opening and closing soundlessly.

"I have to ask," Milton gasped, his voice high-pitched and incredulous. "What is your innovative new design?"

"You can ask, but we haven't finalized all the details yet."

"You haven't finalized . . ." Milton closed his eyes and rubbed a grease-coated back of the hand over his brow, leaving a long streak. "Gentlemen, for twenty years I have worked on my flying wagon design and only now am I ready to bring that project to fruition. And in the next two hours you reckon you'll build something that'll fly."

"One hour," Fergal said, holding up a finger. "We've got to let the paint dry first."

"And," Randolph said, "we could do with a rest first. It's been a long day."

Fergal stretched his arms wide and feigned a yawn.

"Yeah, and all that flying will be tiring and we need to build up our strength."

"You two," Milton spluttered, "are . . . are . . . are . . ."

"Are idiots," Ezekiel offered.

"I was going to say, are looking at a very embarrassing failure."

Fergal looked up at the airship. "Yeah, and I'm looking at one right now."

"Failure! Failure!" Milton advanced on Fergal, his small fists rising, but faced with a scientist who was smaller than himself, Fergal stood his ground, and it was Ezekiel who clamped a hand on Milton's shoulder and pulled him back.

"Leave these idiots to their deluded dreams. We'll have all the revenge we want when their flying wagon gets as far as we all know it will."

"Which is," Fergal said, pointing to the hill opposite, "to the other side of the lake before yours does."

Milton stood a moment, but after a roll of his shoulders and a pat on the back from Ezekiel, he headed back to his flying wagon.

Ezekiel looked at Fergal, his eyes narrowing to streaks of ice, but then shrugged and headed after him, leaving Fergal and Randolph to exchange a smile then flop down on the back of their wagon to enjoy their belated dinner.

As Milton barked orders to his helpers, Randolph passed Fergal a heel of bread.

"Perhaps Milton was right," he said. "It might take more than an hour to build our flying wagon."

"Nah," Fergal said between mouthfuls, "it won't take long, and anyhow, that paint really ain't dry yet."

They watched Milton fuss around the balloon as it slowly filled out, taking on the shape of a giant cylinder and, to a great roar from the watching crowd, rose even higher. As the flying wagon hovered, its great shadow spread out to envelop most of the hill, but on the edge of that shadow, Randolph and Fergal were licking their fingers clean.

"You reckon we should start now?" Fergal asked.

Randolph patted his stomach and stretched.

"That mean you're rested now?"

"Yup." Fergal glanced at the buckboard. "But the paint still looks damp."

"Better give it another half-hour then."

They sat back and, with their hands locked behind their heads, watched Milton's army of helpers attach the metal-framed cradle to the balloon. Then they released most of the stays that were holding the structure down. With stately grace, it rose another thirty feet into the air, dragging the cradle two feet off the ground and leaving just four main ropes to secure the flying wagon.

"That sure is a thing of beauty," Fergal said with genuine admiration in his voice.

"It is, but watching it ain't getting our flying wagon built."

"It ain't, but do you really need me? I'm kind of enjoying watching all this activity."

Randolph shrugged. "I guess not. I've still got thirty minutes to build a flying wagon. I guess it don't need two of us. You admire the view."

"I will." Fergal watched Randolph turn the buckboard round and drag it behind the wagon so that it was out of sight of Milton and Ezekiel.

Hammering and sawing sounds emerged from behind the wagon. Buck and Hodge wandered closer to see what Randolph was doing, but Fergal shooed them away, leaving only Pegasus to occasionally look up from his feeding to watch Randolph, shake his mane, then return to munching.

Milton shouted out a series of orders to everyone and, when he received affirmatives, he and Ezekiel hurried over to the flying wagon. So in response Fergal clicked his fingers and, from behind his wagon, Randolph hurried out to join him and stand before them.

"You ready at last?" Randolph asked, stretching.

"There isn't a breath of wind now," Milton said. "So I'm ready but are you?"

"Sure am."

Ezekiel set his hands on his hips and favored Randolph with a sneer.

"But," he said with heavy sarcasm in his voice, "don't you have checks to carry out first?"

"Nope. We're confident it'll work first time."

Randolph glanced at Fergal, who raised his hand, but then lowered it and looked at Ezekiel.

"And the rules of this wager," Fergal said, "are that the first person to get from here to the other side of the lake without touching the water is the winner?"

Ezekiel rubbed his jaw as he considered Fergal, and shrugged.

"As long as no part of the flying wagon touches the water either."

Fergal nodded then gestured to Randolph, who led Pegasus behind the wagon. Low muttering emerged as Randolph hitched up Pegasus to the buckboard.

Then he appeared, driving the buckboard. At first glance, it was no different to the buckboard that had gone behind the wagon, but it did have a tangle of ropes around the seat and splayed out over the sides.

"Our flying wagon," Fergal announced, throwing his thin arms wide to reveal his bright green waistcoat. "The finest flying wagon there has ever been or ever will be."

"But," Milton murmured, "it's still just your buckboard."

"Not just any buckboard. We've painted it."

"As you said, but paint will not get it off the ground."

Fergal pointed at the picture on the side.

"And it's got an eagle on the side."

"An eagle on the side will not get it off the ground either."

"Then show them how it works, Randolph."

"What now?" Randolph said, pulling the buckboard to a halt facing the lake. "Shouldn't we wait until the race?"

"No, let Milton see what he's up against and maybe he'll give up."

"Yeah," Milton said, folding his arms. "Show me what I'm up against."

"Well," Randolph said, standing, "we've based our design on watching birds in flight and we reckon we've understood the principle of flying."

"I watched birds when I was a child and I quickly realized that the dynamics of bird flight would never work for man-made flight." Milton shook his head, sighing. "But amaze me. Show me what I missed during my twenty years of patient research."

Randolph nodded then pulled hard on the ropes. The two central boards on the sides of the buckboard pivoted out until they were pointing out at right angles. Then he yanked back and forth on the ropes, waggling the two boards in a fair approximation of flapping wings.

For their part, Ezekiel, Milton, and the rest of the crowd stared at the flapping wagon with their mouths open. Then someone laughed, and that opened the floodgates to unrestrained hilarity.

Five minutes later, Milton had composed himself enough to speak again. Most of the other observers were still clutching their sides and trying to draw breath.

"And you reckon," Milton said between laughs, "that your flapping wagon will provide you with enough elevation to keep you airborne, do you?"

"Yeah," Randolph said, pouting with his hands on his hips.

"And how will you control the three axes of flight?"

"What do you mean by axes?"

"Roll, pitch and yaw." Milton watched Randolph shrug, then placed his hand flat and rocked it from side to side. "How will you avoid tumbling over when you're in the air?"

"We don't aim to do no tumbling over in the first place."

"You might not, but with no ground to support you, you could overbalance."

Randolph slapped the seat beside him. "We aim to sit on either side of this here seat and balance each other out."

Milton glanced at the bulky Randolph, then at the thin Fergal.

"But you're different weights. A gust of wind might force you to fall to one side."

"If that happens, we'll swap places."

Milton closed his eyes a moment. A mixture of a pained screech and a gulp slipped from his lips.

"An ingenious solution. And the final issue—how will you get enough thrust?"

Randolph narrowed his eyes. "Thrust?"

"I mean the force to get you off the ground. Or will that moth-eaten bay do that for you?"

"It will." With his arm outstretched, Randolph mimed the wagon hurtling down the slope then sailing into the air over the lake. "Pegasus will get us enough speed, and the rest is down to our secret design."

"Which is?"

Randolph flinched. "I'm not demonstrating that on account of me not wanting to get in the air before the race starts."

Milton turned to his flying wagon, shaking his head.

"Then I'll look forward to seeing it," he called over his shoulder, "from about twenty feet above your heads."

"And I'm looking forward," Ezekiel said, "to seeing you hand over your wagon and all its contents."

"And I'm looking forward," Fergal said, "to seeing you hand over the prize money."

Ezekiel snorted. "This is one wager I am just not losing."

Fergal bit his bottom lip, suppressing a smile, then joined Randolph on the front of the buckboard.

Ezekiel stood a moment, shaking his head, then hurried after Milton.

"You ready to fly, Fergal?" Randolph asked.

Fergal gave the wings an experimental flap.

"As I'll ever be."

Randolph rolled his shoulders. "Then let's get this race won."

Randolph edged Pegasus forward to the edge of the slope before the lake, about thirty yards ahead of Milton's flying wagon and to its side.

"You don't mind," Fergal called to Milton, "if we start from here, do you?"

"You can start anywhere you like!" Milton shouted from the cradle. "You'll still end up in the lake!"

Then Milton started his final checks. After receiving affirmatives from all quarters, he gestured to Buck and Hodge to join him in the cradle. Then he gestured to each of the men standing beside the stays that were holding the balloon down. Each man returned a thumbs-up and raised their axes, ready to cut through the ropes simultaneously.

With this agreement, Ezekiel stood on a podium and gestured to the crowd for quiet.

"Today," he announced, his eyes and teeth gleaming, his white suit pristine in the afternoon sun, "Ezekiel T Montgomery invites you to witness both the sublime and the ridiculous." He pointed to Fergal and Randolph. "Those two idiots are about to roll into the lake headfirst, where they will probably break their necks and drown. But Milton Moon will soar and swoop high above them as he takes his flying wagon on its maiden voyage. You've never seen anything like it, but that's what you expect from the greatest showman alive."

Ezekiel clapped his hands high above his head and, with a coordinated ripple of activity, the workers swung their axes on the ropes, severing them.

Despite themselves, Randolph and Fergal dragged in a deep breath. Although they, like everyone else, expected the flying wagon to hurtle into the air, or plummet to the ground, or at least do something, it just stayed precisely where it was.

An expectant gulp echoed around the crowd, as an uncertain moment lengthened where nobody knew whether the flying wagon would work, or if disaster would befall. But then Randolph saw that it was rising after all. Its pace was slow and it was difficult to spot the moment when it stopped moving but Milton had predicted it would rise twenty feet and to Randolph that seemed about right.

Then Buck and Hodge started bobbing up and down in the cradle as they cranked. Their efforts rocked the cradle back and forth. The blades at the back of the cradle revolved and, with another almost imperceptible movement, the flying wagon moved off.

It didn't swoop and it didn't soar, but nobody within the crowd complained as it quietly glided overhead, heading toward the lake at a pace that would have embarrassed Pegasus.

Randolph and Fergal rocked their heads forward to watch it sail over them, then swung round to watch the cradle head past them.

Inside, Milton shouted orders to Buck and Hodge, which were mainly urges for them to wind faster. And they probably heeded him because the flying wagon speeded up to walking pace then swung to the side as Milton pivoted the blades at the back to steer it on a straighter course for the lake.

The crowd hurried down the slope beneath the flying wagon and hurled their hats in the air. Some hats brushed the underside of the cradle and this encouraged Milton to peer over the side, but he only waved everyone on, encouraging them to see if they could throw a hat all the way up to him. Nobody succeeded, so Milton dangled over the back of the cradle and hailed Fergal.

"I'm flying!"

"We can see that!" Fergal shouted. "And congratulations!"

"And don't go drowning yourself on account of some stupid wager. I tried all the ridiculous ways to fly when I was younger. And I just got myself a whole heap of bruises for my trouble."

"Thanks for the advice but we have our own plan."

"Then if you don't drown I'll give you a ride later."

Randolph and Fergal exchanged a wink.

"You will," Fergal whispered, then turned to face the smiling Ezekiel, who paced to the side of the buckboard, appraising it with a gleam in his eye.

"You not flying yet?" he asked.

"We're going in another minute."

"Why not go now?"

Fergal raised a finger. "Milton got us thinking. Perhaps we do need some last-minute checks."

"The only check you need is whether this flying wagon floats."

"It doesn't. But give us some room. We're starting our final checking procedure."

"I'll stay precisely where I am." Ezekiel set his feet wide and grinned. "I reckon this should be fun."

Fergal shrugged then turned and nudged Randolph.

"Flapping mechanism ready?" he asked.

Randolph flapped the boards on the side, forcing Ezekiel to duck. He waited until Ezekiel stood, then dragged them back, but Ezekiel had anticipated the move and smoothly ducked out of the way again.

"Check."

"Elevation device ready?"

Randolph lifted the rope from his lap and waved it.

"Check."

"Starting mechanism ready?"

Randolph shook the reins. "Check."

"Stopping mechanism ready?"

Randolph thought for a moment, then shook the reins again.

"Check."

"Flying wagon taken on all its fuel?"

Randolph glanced at Pegasus, then yanked the reins to drag its head up from the grass.

"Just finished."

"Thousand dollar prize ready?"

"You'd better ask Ezekiel."

Fergal looked at Ezekiel, receiving a loud guffaw in return, then faced the front.

"Check."

Randolph glanced up at Milton's flying wagon, which was now about thirty yards from the edge of the lake.

"Then let's get this flying wagon in the air."

He shook the reins and Pegasus trundled off down the slope at a walking pace. They both turned to wave over their shoulders at Ezekiel, receiving only a wide and incredulous grin in return. Then they shuffled round to face down the slope and the lake beyond. Their walking pace built up to a slow trot, then a fast trot.

As the slope steepened, Randolph shook the reins hard and Pegasus had no choice but to almost break into a gallop as it hurried after Milton's flying wagon and even started to gain on it.

"Ready with stage one?" he asked as above them, the front of the flying wagon edged over the water.

"Ready," Fergal said, lifting the rope from his lap.

Randolph counted down from three then gestured to Fergal, who pulled hard on the rope, releasing the rigging and leaving Pegasus to trot to a halt. But the slope made them veer off and they hurtled down the hill toward the flattened rock and the ten-foot drop into the lake. Now, with each turn of the wheels, they were gaining on the flying wagon.

"Are we going fast enough this time?" Fergal shouted, gripping the seat on either side of him to avoid the frantic rocking of the buckboard throwing him to the ground.

"Hope so," Randolph grunted, the bone-jarring pace making his teeth rattle. "We can't go no faster."

Fergal gave the wings a flap, hoping that might give them an extra burst of speed, but they rumbled over a stone and the jarring motion snapped the rope from his hand. The right wing fell off.

Randolph glanced back to watch the wing roll to a halt, then up the slope where the crowd had lined the edge to watch their foolhardy attempt to fly. Most were laughing. Pegasus even broke off from searching for fresh grass to watch them hurtle toward the lake, but whether he was worrying about them or the buckboard, Randolph couldn't tell. Then he snapped round to the front to find that they were just thirty yards from the water.

Ahead, half of the flying wagon was over the lake, the cradle swinging free above the water, the first sliver of the vast bulk of the dirigible's reflection visible in the water from the pursuing horseless buckboard.

"You got any last words," Randolph shouted, "before we start flying?"

"Aside from we've only got one shot at this, so aim right, nope."

Randolph nodded then kicked the second wing away. He dragged the rope into his lap, while Fergal kicked back under the seat, freeing the stays that connected the seat to the buckboard.

With nothing to hold them down, they bounced along for the last ten yards, the wind ripping into their faces as the buckboard trundled down the slope faster than it had ever traveled before. The wheels protested, screeching and cracking, and a huge bounce over a rock convinced Randolph that the wheels would come off at any moment, but he forced that worry from his mind to concentrate on his most important task.

He pulled back the rope, playing out the noose he'd hidden beneath the coils, then swung the makeshift lasso over his head, widening the circle with every trundled yard nearer the lake. Then, just as they hit the flat area of rock and were within feet of plummeting into the water, he threw the lasso. It arced out, sailing over the water and straight for the flying wagon.

Numerous projections were on the back of the cradle and Randolph reckoned he'd be unlucky if he missed them all, but his lasso caught the one he'd aimed for, which was about ten feet behind the whirling blades.

Then the buckboard's front wheels hurtled over the edge of the rock, the rear wheels following a moment later. For a moment, Randolph's stomach felt as if it came up into his mouth and he had the distinct impression that he was flying. Then gravity defeated the speed of the buckboard and it nose-dived into the water.

But Fergal and Randolph didn't join it as they sailed on, their unhitched seat now attached to the back of the flying wagon. They swung on a great arc, sitting on the seat with both men clutching the back to avoid being thrown into the water that rushed by them, about ten feet below.

From below, they heard a huge splash as the buckboard met its inevitable end. And from above, they heard Milton shouting as his flying wagon protested with a huge grinding of metal. They ignored him and concentrated on keeping their balance as the seat swung to a halt at the extent of its swing, all the time accompanied by enough screeching to suggest both flying wagons would end up in the water.

Again, Randolph's stomach lurched and both he and Fergal uttered a strangulated scream. Then they were swinging backwards. Randolph glanced down at the water that was rushing past them in the opposite direction.

"This flying sure makes you queasy!" he shouted.

"Yeah! It'll never catch on!"

Randolph laughed, but this time, they didn't swing back as far as they'd swung forward and, with a certain gentle style, they swung to a halt beneath the cradle. Not that the flying wagon above them was taking their maneuver without complaint. The metal frame was still creaking so loudly it sounded as if it'd break at any moment, and Milton was urging Buck and Hodge to compensate for their extra weight. As sand cascaded around them, Randolph glanced over the side to see that the water was closer than it had been before, perhaps eight feet away, then over his shoulder.

The edge of the water was about thirty yards back. Up the slope, the crowd was gesturing at them and Randolph tried to pick out Ezekiel. He saw that a man in a white costume was jumping up and down on the spot and assumed that this was Ezekiel, then looked up. He cringed.

There was no mistaking Milton, and no mistaking that he wasn't pleased as he dangled over the edge of the cradle, his face bright red as he shook a fist at them.

And in his other hand, he was clutching a large knife.

Chapter Thirteen

"**H**owdy!" Randolph shouted, raising his hat. "We thought we'd take you up on that offer of a ride on your flying wagon."

"That offer wasn't meant for this journey," Milton spluttered. "And what do you think you're trying to achieve here?"

"We're flying."

"I am flying. You are hanging on."

"I believe," Fergal said, "the race winner is the first person to reach the other side of the lake without getting his feet wet, whether he gets there by flying or by hanging on."

"That wasn't what was meant."

"But it was what I agreed with Ezekiel. And I sure feel like I'm flying." Fergal looked at the water below, then sat back in the seat with his hands tucked behind his head and his legs stretched out. "And I ain't getting my feet wet before I set foot on the other side before you."

"Then I've got news for you! You'll be getting all of you very wet soon. I designed this flying wagon for three people and your weight will wreck it long before we reach the other side."

Randolph and Fergal peered over the side. Randolph judged that the water was now only seven feet below them and they weren't even a quarter of the way across the lake.

Fergal snapped back up. "Then crank faster."

"The cranking doesn't control our height, just our speed. And unless you jump off, we'll all end up in the water."

"I will not. I can't swim."

"Then I suggest you learn. I haven't got that much ballast to offload." Milton hurled a bag over the side, then darted his head back into the cradle. "Buck, I'll crank. You cut their rope."

Buck swung over the side of the cradle with Milton's knife clutched between his teeth. He was thirty feet above them and would need to crawl for ten feet along two parallel poles while avoiding the revolving blades to reach the rope.

"Stop him," Fergal urged. "I really can't swim."

Randolph jumped to his feet, swayed, his motion rocking the seat to the side. Then hand over hand he pulled himself up the rope with his feet locked on either side of it. His frantic movements made Buck sway and slow his progress, so he yanked the rope back and forth even harder.

Fergal urged him on, but Buck crawled on until he was within an arm's length of the rope. By then Randolph was close enough to see the gleam in Buck's eye as he yanked the knife from his mouth and swung the blade.

Randolph lunged and grabbed hold of Buck's arm before the knife cut into the rope, then pushed him away. Buck wheeled his arms for balance, but a quick yank on the rope was all it took to make him tumble backward and splash into the water.

Randolph watched Buck flounder, confirming he could swim, then pulled himself up to the poles. He expected Hodge to come for him now but the encumbered flying wagon made enough noise to mask Buck's cries and so he reached the cradle unnoticed.

He faced a surprised Hodge and punched at him before Hodge could gather his wits. He'd aimed for his nose but Hodge rocked back and the blow landed short, leaving Randolph with an arm thrust out.

Hodge moved to grab that arm but Randolph saw his intent and yanked it away. Hodge's left hand crunched into the metal frame. As he screeched and wrung his hand, Randolph vaulted into the cradle.

Milton had raised his hands and was showing no sign of getting involved in a fight. So Randolph turned but he walked into Hodge's right hook to the chin and his flailing blow to the cheek that rocked him into the side. He clung on, looking down at Fergal, who was now just five feet from the water and gesturing wildly for him to deal with Hodge quickly.

"Stop fighting!" Milton shouted as the cradle shuddered. "You'll bring us all down!"

Hodge had raised a substantial fist ready to hit Randolph again but Milton's comment distracted him, giving Randolph enough time to right himself then easily duck under his flailing blow. With a surge of delight in his heart, Randolph barged Hodge away into the rudder, which snapped off in his hand and so when he came at Randolph again he was swinging the metal bar before him.

Randolph jerked back, feeling the draft of Hodge's huge first swipe waft past his nose. Then, with Hodge off-balance, he kicked him in the side, folding him over the central crank. Hodge somersaulted before landing on his back, the rudder falling from his grasp. Randolph didn't give him a chance to regain his breath and hoisted him off the floor then hurled him over the side.

"I don't know what your intentions are," Milton said, raising his hands toward Randolph as a splash and Fergal's cry of triumph sounded below, "but stay away from me."

"I've got no desire to throw you into the water

after Hodge. I just want to help you get this flying wagon to dry land."

"To win the wager?"

"Yeah, but also to prove your invention works." Randolph glanced up at the green and red expanse above him. "And it'd be a shame if it didn't."

"I guess it would at that."

Randolph looked over the side to the see that with the reduction in weight, they were rising, and the wagon wasn't creaking so much any more.

"So," he said, grabbing the crank, "do you want me to crank? Or are we just going to stay in the middle of this lake forever?"

Milton flashed a smile. "Crank."

Randolph nodded and began a steady circular motion on the crank.

Milton rummaged around on the floor, locating the rudder, then re-attached it. He declared himself content that he could steer, then considered Randolph, who was gradually increasing the speed of his whirling until his arms were pistoning back and forth and his elbows were creaking.

"How fast are we going?" Randolph shouted.

Milton peered over the side. "Maybe two miles an hour."

"Two miles! That's slower than Pegasus."

"When I had two men cranking, we were going at four miles an hour."

"That sure makes a lot of difference," Randolph

said, then laughed. "And you really reckon there's a use for traveling this slowly?"

"Of course." Milton puffed his chest. "We are flying."

"But we could get there faster by walking." Randolph stopped cranking to look over the side of the cradle. And he saw that most of the crowd were sauntering around the side of the lake and keeping abreast of them.

"This is the first flying wagon entirely powered and steered by man, but it won't be the last."

Randolph stretched his arms, freeing a cramp from his muscles, then started cranking again.

"This is the last flying wagon powered by *this* man."

From the end of the lake, he heard shouting and he glanced ahead to see that Ezekiel had reached the other side ahead of everyone else and he was bellowing and gesturing at them. And the cradle rocked as he presumed that Fergal climbed to his feet to gesture back.

Then Fergal started shouting. Over the grinding of metal, Randolph couldn't hear what either man was saying, but he guessed that the argument about who was actually winning the race was already starting. And it wouldn't be long before they could end it. Even at their dawdling pace, they were already closing on the opposite side of the lake.

He slowed his pumping so that he could hear.

"I hope you have my prize money ready!" Fergal shouted from the seat.

"I am not paying up!" Ezekiel shouted back. "You cheated!"

"I didn't cheat. When I get to the other side first, I won't have got my feet wet. So, I'll have won."

"We agreed that you and Milton would both build a flying wagon and that the first to get across the lake would be the winner."

"And I *did* build a flying wagon." Fergal slapped the seat. "Except mine flew underneath Milton's flying wagon."

"Only because you lassoed the real flying wagon. Your wagon wasn't separate."

Fergal snorted. "Did we set off after Milton?"

Ezekiel coughed and grumbled. "Yeah."

"Did we roll down the hill?"

"Yeah."

"Then we were separate."

Ezekiel muttered to himself. "I guess you could argue that, but you haven't got to the other side yet. And if you even try to get down from that seat my men will blast you in two before you touch the ground."

"Don't shoot!" Milton shouted, then dragged Randolph's hand from the crank.

Randolph looked ahead to see that Ezekiel had lined several of his performers up around him and they'd aimed their guns at Fergal.

"Then stop right there!" Ezekiel shouted, looking up at Milton.

"We've stopped!" Milton shouted back. "And don't shoot. The gas is highly flammable. We'll all be killed."

"Don't worry. My men are precision shooters, and your flying wagon ain't the target."

As Fergal interrupted to trade insults with Ezekiel, Randolph glanced at Milton.

"What can we do?" he asked.

"I'm not doing anything to encourage this argument if there's any danger of bullets getting fired." Milton glanced at the crank. "Start cranking. I'll steer us back across the lake."

"But we haven't reached the other side yet."

Milton pointed upwards. "If one of Ezekiel's men shoots at us and misses, the explosion will blast us all so high we'll probably land in Harvest Pass!"

"Explosion!" Randolph said, shaking his head. "I really can't see this flying becoming popular."

Milton muttered to himself while pushing the rudder as far to the right as possible, and Randolph started cranking.

Below them, Fergal and Ezekiel continued to shout at each other, but the flying wagon was arcing round to run parallel to the lake's edge, and heading back across the water.

Then Fergal screeched.

Randolph looked down, searching around until he

saw what had frightened Fergal. Hodge had emerged from the water and was stomping through the shallow water, his clothes sodden and dangling off him.

"We've got to get more height!"

"We can't!" Milton shouted. "This is as high as we'll go!"

While still cranking, Randolph hung over the side of the cradle and watched Hodge take a run and a jump at the seat. He grabbed hold of the bottom, forcing the flying wagon to lurch as his extra weight dragged them down.

Fergal kicked out, trying to knock Hodge's hands away, but Hodge swung himself up and flopped on to the seat beside him. Fergal slapped both his hands on Hodge's back at the same moment that Hodge grabbed his legs and both men struggled, each trying to throw the other into the water.

On dry land, Ezekiel urged Hodge on and, with the rest of the performers offering their own catcalls, Hodge grabbed Fergal's collar and shook him.

Randolph shouted advice down at Fergal, but this only encouraged Hodge to slug Fergal's jaw and send him spinning into the rope.

Fergal clung on, then glanced up and nodded. He jumped up and grabbed the rope above his head. He thrust his legs down, gaining height on Hodge, who lunged for his trailing feet, but he missed and toppled himself off the seat to land with a huge splash in the shallows.

He stood up, muddy water cascading from his form, and waded after the seat, but Randolph cranked as hard as he could. So, by the time Hodge reached the seat, the water was up to his waist and even when he jumped as high as he could, his fingers could only brush the bottom of the seat.

Fergal continued to climb the rope to reach the cradle.

"Why is he still climbing up to us?" Milton said.

Randolph looked around, then winced. He pointed to the side where Sheriff Johnson was galloping around the lake toward Ezekiel.

"To get away from the sheriff." Randolph sighed. "We've been walked out of town three times this week. I guess Fergal doesn't fancy being flown out this time."

Chapter Fourteen

Sheriff Johnson dragged his horse to a halt. He barely glanced at the flying wagon hovering over the lake and Fergal climbing the rope beneath before he turned to the assembled crowd.

"Bank raid!" he shouted. "Bandits have raided the bank."

"Van Romalli?" Ezekiel asked.

"Got no idea. But they've got away with everything."

Ezekiel winced and, within seconds, he was organizing his performers and the on-lookers to form a posse and, within less than a minute, everyone had mounted their horses.

In the flying wagon, Randolph stopped cranking so that he could see whether any of them would stay behind to continue fighting over the result of the race, but Hodge and Buck emerged from the water and mounted horses.

Nobody else as much as looked at them as they organized themselves then galloped after Sheriff Johnson toward Harvest Pass.

Fergal rolled over the side of the cradle in time to look down and see the newly deserted side of the lake.

"They've all gone?" he said.

"Yeah," Randolph said. "But I guess you knew that'd happen."

"Yeah. I did a deal with those bandits." Fergal flashed a smile. "The information I bought our freedom with was that everyone would be here watching the race, leaving the town deserted and the bank unguarded."

"I guess I can't complain too much if that means we can leave town without being raided." Randolph turned to Milton. "What you want to do now?"

Milton glanced around then pointed back across the lake.

"Might as well head back to dry land. All my equipment is back there and I have nothing left to prove up here."

As Randolph started cranking, he peered at the departing posse.

"And let's hope they catch Van Romalli."

"They won't," Milton said, edging the rudder to

the side to steer a straight course across the lake. "Van Romalli isn't part of that bandit gang."

Randolph broke off from cranking a moment to glance at Fergal, and saw Fergal nodding.

"How do you both know that?"

"I met the bandits," Fergal said. "And they admitted they had nothing to do with Romalli." He turned to Milton. "But how do you know that?"

"Sheriff Johnson talks a lot. He told me about that cryptic message Morgana Sullivan left you: When Van Romalli has gone only Angus is left."

"And you figured out what it means?"

"It wasn't that cryptic." Milton shrugged. "Well, not for a man who has an aptitude for solving anagrams."

"And the answer?" Fergal asked. He stared at Milton but when Milton just smiled, he spread his arms. "We'll share the reward money if you tell us."

Milton looked around Fergal to stare at the approaching lakeside.

"But I believe the reward for providing information that'll lead to the capture of Van Romalli will go to whoever provides that information."

"Yeah."

Milton tapped his chest. "And that person is me. I've already told Marshal Jim Broughton what I suspect."

Fergal sighed. "Then just so I know, what did it mean?"

"I think you'll work it out soon enough." Milton pointed then nodded, signifying that Randolph and Fergal should see what was ahead.

Randolph turned and saw that the flying wagon was about one hundred yards from the side of the lake, their half-submerged buckboard appearing ahead.

But further up the slope, a rider was hurrying along toward Pegasus. Randolph narrowed his eyes and, as the form drew alongside the horse, he discerned it as being Morgana Sullivan.

Without any complaint from the bow-legged bay, Morgana led it away, but instead of heading back along the direction from which she'd come, she headed straight for their wagon.

"I just knew she wouldn't repay our kindness," Fergal grumbled. "Milton, get this wagon to the side."

"We're going as fast as we can."

"No, we ain't!" Randolph shouted, pausing from his cranking to glare at Fergal and, getting the hint, Fergal joined him and grabbed the metal.

Fergal's wild pumping added little in the way of extra speed, but the companionable encouragement helped Randolph to put on a burst of speed.

But as they reached the side of the lake, Morgana had already hitched up her own horse and Pegasus to the wagon and was climbing on to their wagon. She gave them a cheery wave then shook the reins, hurrying the two horses on.

"Angus, away!" she shouted.

Up in the cradle, Randolph glanced at Fergal.

"Angus, she just called the horse Angus."

"Of course she did," Milton said, then raised his eyebrows. "Van Romalli and Angus are a team."

"What do you mean?"

"If you put Angus and Van Romalli together, then juggle the letters, what do you get?"

"Don't know."

"Morgana Sullivan. Morgana *is* Van Romalli."

"But Van Romalli is a ruthless outlaw with a scar on his . . ."

"I've heard that nobody has seen him before." Milton shrugged. "And what better disguise for an outlaw is there than being a woman when everyone is looking for a man?"

"I guess none," Fergal grumbled then slapped his forehead.

"Quit talking, Milton," Randolph shouted, "and turn this wagon and head after her!"

Despite the futility of this gesture, Milton slammed the rudder hard to the right. At their painfully slow speed, they edged out over dry land.

Below them, Morgana watched them approach, then shook the reins, encouraging the horses to speed to a walking pace.

In the cradle, Fergal and Randolph pumped as fast as they could, also getting the wagon up to walking pace then beyond as they embarked on a pursuit of the permanently slow Pegasus. But Morgana had the nerve to steer the wagon down the slope then along the side of the lake so that it was in their path.

"She's taunting us," Fergal grunted as he bobbed up and down.

"I don't care," Randolph snapped, cranking hard. "Pegasus is the slowest horse I've ever seen and she'll pay for that arrogance when we catch her."

"And do you reckon Pegasus will get tired before our arms fall off?" Fergal pumped one last time then slumped over the crank, his arms dangling and his brow wet, but Randolph was cranking with so much vigor he dragged him off his feet and the rhythm shook Fergal into helping again.

"We'll catch her. I know Pegasus and he's had a tiring day."

Milton glanced over the side to relay that they were now directly behind Morgana and only fifty yards away, then forty-five.

But despite Randolph's optimism, he really was feeling as if he was in danger of losing his arms if he continued pumping. So, when they'd closed to within thirty yards, he had no choice but to swap places with Milton.

The flying wagon slowed, but even with the weaker men powering it, they were still inching toward Morgana—twenty yards, nineteen . . .

"We've been on some frantic chases to keep our wagon before," Randolph said, massaging his bunched biceps, "but never one at this pace."

"Don't worry," Fergal grunted, breaking off to swipe sweat from his brow. "Even if we're crawling along, we're catching up on her."

Randolph leaned over the side to watch the dirigible edge forward to hover over the wagon.

Slowly, Morgana came into view on the seat. She was peering up while shaking the reins, but even though Pegasus was still just bumbling along and they were within seconds of being above her, she was smiling and even waved again.

"She don't appear worried," Randolph said.

Fergal snorted. "She will be when we get back our wagon."

The dangling seat nudged into the back of the wagon and Randolph was judging whether he should slide down the rope and climb on to the back of the wagon when Morgana flinched and looked to her side. She peered that way a moment, then shook the reins with more vigor.

Randolph looked to the side to see what had worried her.

Marshal Jim Broughton and Deputy Lloyd Henderson were galloping around the side of the lake and heading straight for her, but they were still more than a half-mile away.

"They took their time," Milton murmured.

Morgana shook the reins again and, just as Randolph was snorting at the unlikelihood of her getting any more speed out of Pegasus, she glanced up at Randolph and grinned.

"Angus," she shouted, "go!"

Both horses pricked up their ears then broke into a fast gallop that hurtled the wagon along the side of the lake. Within moments, the wagon was free of the chasing flying wagon and within ten seconds it already had one hundred yards on them.

Randolph hung his head a moment, then signaled that Fergal and Milton should relent from their pumping.

Both men didn't need any further encouragement to stop, and they shuffled round to join Randolph, grumbling as they rubbed their tired muscles.

But that grumbling intensified when they saw the receding wagon.

"I guess we just didn't know the right thing to say to get Pegasus moving," Randolph said. "I mean Angus."

Fergal sighed as he slapped a hand against the crank.

"This has to be the worst day of my life," he said. "I've let myself be double-crossed by Morgana Sullivan again."

"It's worse than that," Randolph muttered, watching Pegasus gallop away like a three-year-old stallion. "We've been double-crossed by a horse."

"Well, you did say that Pegasus was either the most stupid animal you've ever met or the most clever." Fergal snorted a harsh laugh as he lowered his head. "But you never mentioned devious."

Randolph narrowed his eyes, then laughed. "I'll settle for something else—loyal."

Fergal looked up to see what Randolph meant and smiled as he saw that Pegasus had veered from the trail and was heading toward the lake.

Morgana was tugging on the reins and encouraging him to head away from his disastrous course. But with the obstinacy that had irritated Fergal and Randolph over the last few days, Pegasus was ignoring her and was even building up more speed as he neared the water.

Then he splashed into the lake. He trundled the wagon on for twenty yards, then slowed to a halt and planted his bow-legs wide. He raised his head to face the flying wagon and whinnied as the water rippled around the wagon, reaching almost to the tops of the wheels.

Morgana screamed at the horses to move, but Pegasus' obstinacy had spread to the other horse and neither of them was going anywhere.

Fergal rolled his shoulders and, with Randolph, resumed cranking while Milton directed the balloon to take the shortest route to the wagon across the water. But Randolph was tired now, and they were still more than a hundred yards from the wagon and advancing on it at a snail's pace.

Farther around the lake, the two lawmen were still galloping on and they would reach her within a minute.

One last time Morgana shook the reins, receiving only a whinny in response, then threw down the reins and leapt into the water. With her skirts hitched up, she waded through the shallows and straight for the dangling seat.

The wagon was nudging over the edge of the water and Milton pushed the rudder hard to the side to direct it away from her, but she continued running and within seconds, reached the seat. She took a running leap and grabbed the edge of the seat, then rolled on to it.

Randolph and Fergal raised their hands from the crank and, as the flying wagon glided to a halt, Morgana shouted a demand that they hurry.

Fergal glanced over the side and shook a fist down at her.

"We aren't going nowhere." He pointed at the approaching lawmen. "But you are going to jail."

"You will get me away from them, now!"

Fergal raised his hands. "We're not helping you no more. You can—"

Fergal flinched, falling into Randolph's chest. Randolph stood him upright but then a gun blast from below sent all three men to hurling themselves to the base of the cradle.

When long seconds had passed and an explosion still hadn't come, they each peered out from under the arms they'd thrown over their heads. Milton was the first to jump to his feet and dangle over the side.

"Do not fire!" he shouted.

Another gunshot blasted. Milton cringed, then glanced up.

Randolph saw a tear appear in the silk, but they were lucky again and the gas didn't ignite.

"Get moving!" Morgana shouted. "Or I'll fire again!"

"We won't be lucky for a third—" Milton cringed away, then gestured for Randolph and Fergal to crank. As they put their hands to the metal, he peered back over the side. "We're doing it. We're moving. Don't fire!"

"Go faster and I won't!"

"We will, but just don't fire. This whole flying wagon could explode and you won't survive down there either."

Morgana muttered more threats from below, but Milton continued to placate her as the flying wagon glided out over the lake. She had just agreed not to fire again when the lawmen drew to a halt at the side of the lake, about thirty yards from the receding seat.

They jumped down from their horses and paced to

the edge of the water to watch them sail out over the lake on the slowest getaway in history.

"Milton," Randolph said, "what do we do now? We're pumping as fast as we can, but the lawmen can just walk around the lake and wait for us no matter which way we go."

"There's not much we can do," Milton said. "There's only one direction this flying wagon is going."

"That way?" Randolph asked, pointing to the other side of the lake.

"Nope." Milton pointed down. "She's blasted a hole in my flying wagon and once the gas escapes, there's no replacing it and we'll lose our buoyancy."

"Meaning?"

"Meaning we'll get lower and lower and lower."

"And Morgana will be in the water?"

"You got it."

Randolph nodded. "Then I guess we should get back to dry land quickly before our passenger drowns."

Milton pushed the rudder hard to the left, redirecting the flying wagon off the lake, but a shot from below ripped out.

The three men winced, glancing up at the flying wagon, then put their hands to their chests.

"I need to talk to her," Milton said. He looked over the side, but Fergal grabbed his arm and pulled him back, then lifted his hand from the rudder and grabbed it himself.

Fergal winked then pushed the rudder to the right to redirect the wagon back toward the center of the lake.

"Perhaps we don't need to head to dry land just yet," he said. "I reckon Morgana could do with cooling off first."

Chapter Fifteen

An hour after the start of the maiden voyage of
Milton Moon's flying wagon, it returned to slowly
deflate over dry land. This was much to the relief of
Morgana Sullivan, who was drenched and wretched
and almost eager to have Marshal Jim Broughton arrest her.

In her dripping wet clothes, she sloshed from the
water toward the two waiting lawmen. Lloyd held a
gun on her while Jim held out a pair of handcuffs but
as a puddle of water grew around her Lloyd shrugged
and wrapped her in a blanket instead.

Jim stood back and hailed Milton in the descend-
ing wagon, then gave a smaller nod to Fergal and
Randolph in acknowledgment of their efforts.

When the cradle was ten feet off the ground,

Randolph jumped down, then secured the trailing rope around a boulder. In the last few minutes, a light breeze had started up and when Fergal joined him, they busied themselves with ensuring the downed flying wagon didn't escape or damage itself.

With Morgana captured, Fergal and Randolph decided to leave as soon as the flying wagon was safe, but the silk envelope was still billowing out and tugging on the ropes they had secured to the ground when the posse returned.

Ezekiel was riding up front and, from his hunched shoulders, Randolph guessed the posse had been unsuccessful in its pursuit of the bandits.

Fergal and Randolph stood before the deflating flying wagon to face the oncoming men. By the side of the lake, the two lawmen were guarding the drying-out Morgana, and Pegasus had pulled the wagon out of the water and returned to his normal activity of tugging up grass.

"I'm on dry land!" Fergal shouted when Ezekiel jumped down from his horse to stand before them. He jumped on the spot to emphasize his point. "And I didn't get my feet wet."

"You will if Hodge throws you in the lake." Behind Ezekiel, Hodge and Buck rolled their shoulders as they grunted their enthusiasm to follow that order. "But it don't matter now. Those bandits got away with everything, including all my takings for the week."

"That sure is terrible for you." Fergal provided a comforting pout, then shrugged. "But you still owe me one thousand dollars."

"I do not." Ezekiel set his hands on his hips. "And we never finished that argument before, but the exact words of our wager were that the first person to reach dry land would win the takings for this show, not that he'd win one thousand dollars. And the bandits took all that money."

Fergal provided a more realistic pout. "Ah, that is most unfortunate."

Ezekiel raised his eyebrows, then gestured back, encouraging Hodge and Buck to flank him.

"It is, but as you've insisted on arguing about the exact terms of our wager, I reckon any sane person would accept you didn't win that race." Ezekiel glanced at Fergal's wagon and grinned, his white teeth providing a dazzling gleam. "I reckon I can sell your wagon and the treasure of Saint Woody to raise some of what I've lost."

Fergal gulped, then provided a hopeful smile.

"Then perhaps we might come to an agreement about our wager."

Randolph paced forward to join Fergal and face Ezekiel's henchmen but Fergal raised a hand, then gestured for Ezekiel to join him by the water. Randolph watched the two men walk away and swing round to face each other. He couldn't hear what they were saying but from the flurry of gestures at each other he judged that a tense negotiation was underway.

Still keeping one eye on them, he joined Milton in helping to secure the flying wagon and ensure it wouldn't blow away.

"You're happy I guess," Randolph said when the silk had flopped down over the cradle.

"My flying wagon worked," Milton said, beaming, then pointed at the two marshals who were leading Morgana away. "I have a two thousand dollar reward for helping to capture Van Romalli. Yeah, I'm happy."

"Glad somebody came out of this with a profit," Randolph said, glancing at Fergal, who was still arguing with Ezekiel.

Milton followed Randolph's gaze. "I guess if Ezekiel insists that you've lost that wager I'll share the reward so you can buy back your wagon."

"Obliged for the offer, but when Fergal starts negotiating I just feel sorry for the other man."

"I think you might be right there."

Milton laughed and then laughed again when Fergal shook hands with the frowning Ezekiel, then paced back from the water, a huge smile appearing.

"We didn't lose everything, then?" Randolph asked, running down the slope toward him.

"Nope." Fergal beckoned Randolph to join him in heading to their wagon. "I persuaded Ezekiel that the result of the race was a tie and that the wager was void."

"How did you do that?"

"I told him how he could make a lot of money from the only attraction that's better than a flying wagon."

Randolph glanced over his shoulder to watch Ezekiel rejoin Hodge and Buck. Ezekiel slapped both men on the shoulders, then shooed them away to give him room. Then he danced round on the spot, miming throwing punches, then being hit, then falling over.

Hodge and Buck furrowed their brows, but when Ezekiel jumped on the buckboard seat and mimed kicking dozens of imaginary foes off it, slow smiles spread.

"And what's better than a flying wagon?" Randolph asked.

"A flying wagon with stunts." Fergal patted a bulge in his jacket, then hurried off toward his wagon. "For a tidy sum, I've sold Ezekiel a great idea for an attraction—get two people to slug it out on a seat that's dangling beneath a flying wagon while the wagon is chasing after bandits on the ground. He'll get back all the money he's lost in a week."

"I guess he will." Randolph hurried on to join Fergal. "But Milton won't enjoy having all that going on while he's experimenting with flying."

Fergal jumped on to his wagon. "He got the reward. What more could he want?"

"Nothing I guess."

Randolph joined Fergal and took the reins. Pegasus glanced back at them and nodded. Then, to only the slightest of tugs, he trundled the wagon in an arc that took them by Milton. But despite making peace with Ezekiel, Randolph ensured that he still gave Hodge and Buck a wide berth. He hailed Milton.

"What's wrong?" Milton asked, turning from watching Ezekiel, who was outlining an elaborate fight.

Already Ezekiel had discarded using the buckboard seat and replaced it with the whole buckboard. And, from his grandiose miming, his latest version of the mock-fight would use all of his performers and, Randolph deduced, several wild animals, a burning buckboard and a kidnapped saloon-girl.

"Nothing. We're going now."

"Then I wish you well," Milton said, beaming. "After what you men did today, you'll go down in history."

"After what we did today, we're just glad we didn't go down in the lake." Randolph smiled. "But one thing before we leave—that treasure of Saint Woody. You said you knew how to open the box."

"I did claim that." Milton scratched his chin. "But I guess the solution is simple."

"And what is it?"

Milton smiled. "Ask Saint Woody."

"What?"

"That's the simplest solution, and I always look for those. Find the man who made the box and ask him how to open it. Then you'll know what's in it, if anything."

Fergal sighed. "Obliged for the advice."

"And all for free." With a last cheery wave, Milton turned and joined Ezekiel.

Randolph watched Milton just long enough to see him hang his head when Ezekiel started to describe his plans for the flying wagon's second voyage, then raised the reins.

"Angus, go!" he shouted then shook the reins.

Pegasus didn't move, so Randolph shook the reins with a firmer crack. Still, the horse didn't move so Fergal gestured for Randolph to pass the reins to him. With a shrug Randolph did as asked.

"Come on, Pegasus," Fergal said, his tone light as he gave the reins a slight tug.

Pegasus speeded to a fair trot.

Randolph sighed. "I guess you just have to show it some respect."

"I guess you do at that."

Both men laughed and settled back in their seats. Ahead of them lay the open and bandit-free trail.

"Where are we going?" Randolph asked.

"That-a-way." Fergal pointed ahead. "We've got ourselves a saint to find."